I0561301

Copyright © 2024 Roland Moore

ISBN: 978-1-963933-01-7 (SB)

Moore Substance Publishing
Original publication 2024

Table of Contents

Preface

Have you ever planned, prepared, and hosted a party or cookout at your residence? If so, I don't have to explain the difference between doing EVERYTHING by yourself as opposed to a great group effort. That's what helps potlucks work well. Everyone brings something to the table, so no one is overwhelmed to the point they can't enjoy the fellowship, food, and fun. Not only does it lessen the stress and responsibilities of one individual, but it allows everyone to enjoy diverse delicacies. Typically, the more dissimilar the meal preppers, the better the chances to savor a variety of seasonings, styles, and cooking talents. If you're fortunate, you might get to sample sensational dishes or drinks from various cultures, ethnicities, or similar groups who do things uniquely differently. Who knows, you might even "discover" someone's secret family recipe that otherwise would've never been celebrated. And that my friend is the purpose behind this project. We hope you enjoy the assortment of "chef" selections we've created for your consumption (Don't be greedy, though. By all means, share with others). The servings are accompanied by each author's name. That way, if you're craving seconds, you'll have what you need to find more of their delightful "dishes." If you fail to locate an author's name under the title, then it was written by me. ***The Writers Refuge*** consists of myself, Barry Tyson, Dominic Murphy, and Martin Murphy. No one was told what to write about. I simply asked everyone to bring what they wanted to the proverbial table. That said, enjoy this fantastic flash fiction smorgasbord of sorts.

SN: We aren't responsible for overindulging.

The Writers Refuge

Arne's Recon

Arne crept up and positioned himself amongst the island's hardwood. The waning daylight and canopy provided the perfect cover for the mission. He took a deep breath and exhaled, allowing his chest and shoulders to relax. He was thankful for another chance to do what he was raised to do. The uncontaminated air and vibrant plant blossoms were remarkable. He hadn't seen such natural beauty for quite some time. His planet had been decaying at a disturbing rate, which expedited the strong-arming of a more suitable planet. The southwestern side of the intriguing isle was full of fruit-bearing trees. That type of lush vegetation,

along with the location of the planet, made it an
ideal target for the galactic Vikings to explore
and conquer, as they'd done for many decades.
His instant infatuation with this new world was
interrupted by a melodious cheer that echoed
over parts of the Island, "All hail Hor-Sesh-Oe!
All hail Hor-Sesh-Oe! All hail Hor-Sesh-Oe!!!"
Back focused on the task at hand, he gripped his
main weapon and blended back into his
surroundings. Before the booming chants
receded into the atmosphere, Arne pinpointed
the direction they'd come from. He navigated his
way towards the well-kept entrance of a cavern;
inside were hundreds of cocoons. Against his
wiser judgment, he decided to inspect it from the
inside. He followed indistinguishable sounds like
a stealthy feline, saturated in curiosity. He eased
forward, maintaining a safe distance, then

looked through his scope. There were sparsely covered women, gazing into a hole of luminescent glory, repeatedly bellowing a phrase, which he couldn't understand. Their majestic incantation was soothing and comforting, making Arne feel at home. "Wow," he muttered as he tracked the movements of his targets. He was locked in on them and hadn't noticed the men that were there. Well, what was left of the men. The head and cauterized torso of naked men were missing limbs and hanging from individual contraptions high above the females. They were still alive, mouths sewn shut. Perplexed, he watched the men being removed from the platform, one by one and taken deeper into the cave. What started as a promising new home, full of intriguing, harmonizing women, soon turned into the land of menacing madams.

Erik's Encounter (Day 2)

Erik cruised toward the northeast part of the island's shore and nestled the spacecraft a few feet from the mainland. "No way! That can't be," bedeviled at what appeared to be a female riding a raptor-esque creature as if it were a colt. He tapped the device, double-checked the screen, and reassessed the image. There was nothing there. "Okay, I didn't think so!" It was well past time for a systems upgrade, so glitches had become the norm. But the Vikings' constant conquests, and lack of current resources, hadn't allowed for any. "This isn't the time for false readings or equipment failures!" Erik exclaimed. He then proceeded to the mouth of a small cave, just off the edge of a mound. He observed a few small beasts in the distance, next to a waterfall. He pulled out his scope to look closer. "Ahhh, so that's what it was," he surmised. The raptor-esque creatures looked to be of the equine family. They were all four-legged creatures but some of them stood on two feet, displaying their talons when they ran. "I guess the scanners are working," he thought. Their mouths contained venomous teeth and one swipe of their claws could maim the toughest prey. His battle-hardened character became even more resolute, with his senses heightened. He surveyed a few more areas but knew it'd be best to have daylight on his side, so he called it a night just in case he had to handle some of those predators.

Erik was up, and ready to handle any and everything, before the sun shone on the attractive planet of Amora. He moved with caution across the soft sands, making his way throughout the region. The chameleon-like camouflage he donned helped him stay undetected. His mind, battle skills, and surveillance techniques were superior. There was a reason he was often chosen to lead vital deployments. The day was without incident, until he heard a thudding disturbance, fast approaching from behind. With precision, he retrieved his weapon and rolled forward before pivoting and strafed to his left, only revealing his eyes beneath his surface-adapting gear. Advancing towards him was one of the beasts he had witnessed the night before. A nauseating stench grew stronger as the beast drew nigh, causing him to gag but not lose focus. Just as the beast was about to trample him, he eviscerated it, ending any ill intentions. While its guts continued to paint the brown sands maroon, he heard the faint wail of a woman coming from the same direction that the now-deceased fauna had come from. Scope in hand again, he scurried to the top of the mound and combed the land. His curiosity was piqued when he realized that the scream sounded more like the melody of a love tune, the closer he got. Two beastly creatures were in calamitous pursuit of a fleeing female. Her skin was radiant, and her hair seemed to have a life of its own; it flowed without the aid of a strong breeze. He hastened to her defense, wasting little time covering ground. The creature's focus shifted from her to him. He thought to himself, '*easy prey*.' They were much smaller than the previous one. However, instead of attacking, they shuffled off into a nearby cave, avoiding termination. The curvy woman approached him without trepidation. To be out there with no shoes and marginal clothing, her feet were flawless, and her skin was without blemish.

"I'm Allu-Re," she spoke first. "Thank you for coming. I am grateful and indebted to you."

He was smitten by her beauty and enchanted by her melodious voice. Quite bewildered by her agility to keep away from the beasts, he asked, "How do you survive here with no weapon and those detestable creatures running around?"

Allu-Re deflected his question, and responded, "I'm just glad you were here. I don't know what I would have done without your bravery." She continued, "I've never seen a man as strong and capable as you. Are you an Amorian?"

Erik, confused, answered, "Amorian? No. Are you alone?" The longer he stood in her presence, the deeper he fell. He was captivated by her attractiveness.

"There are many more women, like me," she replied. "Would you like to meet them? We would LOVE to have you."

'MORE like you,' he thought to himself. He had just met the most gorgeous being he'd ever seen, and she claimed there were more just like her. He caught himself before his excitement was evident. "In due time," he retorted. "I can't come tonight, but I will be back very soon. I even plan to bring my friends, if you don't mind, since there's more of you."

"I wouldn't have it any other way!" She made certain that he knew she was stimulated. "But how do I know you'll return, and when?

That way we can be prepared for all of you. I want to make sure it's a meeting we'll always remember."

Her concerned look compelled him to prove that he'd be back. Honestly, if he didn't have to pick Arne up at the rendezvous, he would've gone back with her then.

"Here," he handed her his most valuable possession. It was a golden horseshoe, filled with diamonds. One for each land he'd conquered. He never took it off, not even when he slept.

"And what is this?" she inquired.

"A promise," he answered, then explained its meaning and significance in greater detail.

"Well, in that case," she said, coming closer, "Let's seal the deal with a kiss." Her tongue controlled his mind as she maneuvered it, igniting senses he never knew existed. She'd grabbed his manhood during their embrace, and as she proceeded to dislodge her tasting tool from his tonsils, she added, "Please bring all of this back, so we can exchange it for your priceless horseshoe."

There was NOTHING that was going to stop him from returning to that island. That said, he had to first dislodge himself from her enchanting charm, control his aroused eagerness, and continue the mission.

Subtle Landing (1 Day Earlier)

"Before we split up, I must thank you again for speaking up for me in front of the king," Arne shared with Erik. "And I won't let you down," he promised.

"Respect," Erik nodded his head and bumped his chest twice while replying. "I know you've been dying to get back in the field since the Happy Lands," he added. "And I know you'd do the same for me if the dawn of that day ever arises." At the time of said mishap, no one could've imagined that Arne would have bounced back from the Happy Land fiasco, much less be given an important assignment. His drug and alcohol-induced blunder caused the death of numerous Vikings and even led to their home planet being attacked. He lost his bloodline during those battles and attacks. He even contemplated taking his own life after the slaughtering ceased. The shame was unbearable, yet here he was not only alive but also with an opportunity to scrape up some remnant of redemption if this two-man mission brought back good news to the king. The King who had him beaten to the brink of death, but kept him alive, knowing that living with that huge ignominy would be worse than dying. Best case scenario, his home planet could survive another four months. Worse, and more realistic case, they only had enough resources to survive another six weeks, not factoring in their vulnerability. An attack from an enemy or overzealous nation would ensure their existence was annihilated. "Remember, tonight we spy out the locals from afar, and then tomorrow when daylight prevails, we go inland for a more in-depth survey," Erik reminded Arne.

"Yes sir," Arne responded. "Do what I can from a distance then move in for clearer details tomorrow. Understood." His face was stoic, and his eyes never flinched or veered from Erik. Anyone from the outside looking in would have been clueless to him wanting to atone for his Happy Land sins. But Erik knew better.

"Don't be a hero," Erik added for reinforcement. "Stick to the plan and we'll both make it back home with great news." He knew that Arne wanted to redeem himself and would do whatever to accomplish that, even if it meant breaking protocol and jeopardizing their two-man exploration.

"I just want to find a new home and try to start over," Arne assured him. "Nothing more, nothing less."

Erik waited before he replied, seeing if he'd catch even the slightest break in Arne's demeanor, but there was none. "Ok," he approved. "Then I will see you tomorrow at the same time and location. Until then, No radio communication."

Arne exited the ship, made his way to the southwestern part of the Island, and Erik took off to the north.

Allu-Re's Great News (After Erik's Encounter)

"I have great news!" Allu-Re shared.

"It'd better be great," the Queen interjected. "I was just about to have a guest for dinner. I don't want to leave him hanging around for too long."

Allu-Re responded with confident glee, "I met a man today; a visitor from another planet!"

The queen looked around and after seeing no one asked, "Andddd where exactly is this man, who's from another planet?"

"He's on his way back to his hometown," she answered.

"Ummm, help me out here, darling. I thought I heard you say you had great news. What's so great, except for his sake, about you meeting a man and letting him go back to his planet, instead of bringing him to the Mandate?"

Allu-Re smiled, "My apologies, your highness," then continued, "Allow me to explain. He is what they call a Galactic Viking warrior. He and his comrades seek and conquer new lands. He was scouting our planet when he heard me playing in the fields on the northeast side of the island with Frankie and Fernious. I had taken them out to play and he thought they were hunting me."

"Men," the Queen shook her head. "They always assume you're in some type of trouble and need rescuing." Allu-Re finished telling her everything about Erik, his luxurious horseshoe chain, and when they were returning with the entire fleet. "Excellent, my beloved," the queen gave her approval. "Let us now prepare for the extravagant feast to come!"

Conflict Resolution

Back at the ship, Erik paced back and forth, trying to contain his excitement. He'd returned two hours ahead of schedule, but Arne was now behind. When he saw Arne, he met him at the entrance, "You are late, we should've departed hours ago," he explained. He was eager to bring good tidings back to the king. "We have found our new home! The king will be more than pleased. The island is rich and overflowing with beautiful women. Allu-re told me so."

"Allu-re? An Amorian woman..." Arne interjected, "You were seen by and met a being from this place?" Arne was surprised to hear this news. Erik, a stickler for protocols, had broken some of his own rules.

Erik responded, "Yes, and they are a gift from the gods. Their beauty is unparalleled, and they've been waiting for men like us to come and protect them from the beasts that occupy this territory."

"Are you out of your Viking mind?! This place must be destroyed. We need to report that to the king at once. I have seen these…these things and beasts of which you speak of are one and the same and they're an abomination to the female species." Arne was confounded at Erik's scouting report, and it concerned him. He began to reflect on his past indiscretions and was certain that the king would side with Erik's misguided assessment over his accurate account. "It was our mission to scout out the land and report back what we have found, Erik." Arne raised his voice, respectfully. "You speak of these creatures as if they're refined women." Erik was looking at Arne as if he was inebriated. Arne tried to wrangle Erik back to his senses, grabbing his forearm while he talked, "Get it together! We had ONE job: find a better home." In true

Viking form, he uttered, "Lo, there, do we fight to live in war and die for Valhalla, Brother… But I assure you, this planet is no place for men, not even Viking men."

Unphased by what he believed was a drunken plea, Erik exclaimed, "It sounds like the mead has clouded your judgment brother. Where did you find the strong drink or were narcotics your choice of pleasure? Tell me now!"

Arne, further agitated by Erik's assertion, is convinced he's stricken by something, and must intervene. The entire fate of the Viking nation hinges on their report to the king. "Have you gone mad my brother? I haven't touched the mead or recreational enhancements for many years now. You know this!" Arne stepped back to reexamine Erik's posture, "What have you taken? That's the real question. Did you eat some plant or drink some unknown Amorian substance, while with this woman of yours?"

Appalled at the notion that Arne would accuse him, Erik snatched Arne's collar, and pulled him in, "I swear, Brother, if you've been drinking or messed this mission up, in the least bit, I'll kill you myself. We need this!" He pushed Arne back a few feet, "You're the reason we're here in the first place! I should have never stood up for you. Don't say another word, or I'll stamp your Valhalla passport where you stand." Erik instinctively placed his hand on his weapon.

"It's not what you th…" before Arne could finish his sentence, Erik attacked, swinging at his head; his intentions were plain. "Whoa, whoa, whoa. Please don't do this, brother." He backed up, protecting himself. "We're not at war with each other. We're on the same team."

"Well, you will surely die, Arne the Decapitator. I'm sure you've missed a step. Now you will lose your head."

Although he was a formidable warrior, Arne had neither motive nor desire to fight Erik, but this was bigger than him. Their civilization was on the line. Nevertheless, he still tried to reason with him, "Erik, something is wrong with you and I'm sure it has something to do with those barbaric bit..."

"Fight me, you drunken coward bastard." Erik cut him off mid-sentence and lunged toward him. This time he was met with resistance. Their weapons clashed and sparks flew. Arne pushed Erik, still pleading for him to get a grip, but Erik swung for Arne's abdomen. At this point, Arne had no choice but to engage in all-out combat. He countered, kicked Erik to the ground, and tried to plant a knee to the face, but Erik rolled out of the way. With a downward swing, Arne crushed the ground next to Erik's neck, nearly removing his head. Erik tried to trip Arne, but he jumped over the leg-sweep, and dived at Erik, pinning him to the ground with his razor-sharp sword. It pierced through the outer layer of Erik's garment.

"I don't want to kill you brother, but I will if you swing that sword again. All I want to do is report to King Ivan and let him decide what's best for the nation." Arne, still gauging Erik's mental state, awaited a response. Once Erik nodded in agreement, they both stood up.

"Forgive me, brother. I don't know what came over me. We're better than this. We may disagree, but it should never lead to death." Erik apologized.

Arne felt he had gotten through to him, 'Finally' he thought to himself. He helped Erik up, and they dusted themselves off.

"Let's go home," Erik suggested. "Secure the entrance. I'll start the engines."

'Wonder who the King will believe?' Arne internalized as he made sure the entrance was ready for take-off. Those same thoughts percolated in Erik's mind.

As Arne reached for the latch, everything went dark.

"Sorry, brother. I can't allow you to ruin our chance at a better life." With a blow to the back of his skull, Erik had knocked Arne out. He pushed him off the ship, setting sail for their homeland. "May you be alive upon our return."

Decisions In Fire

Barry Tyson

Marcus stared at the flickering flames in the fireplace. The mantle was a cherry wood with a polished onyx trim that made it look solid and sturdy. It was a direct contrast to the wild dance the fire performed: a tiny, tamed piece of chaos burned inside, capable of destroying everything but contained by its designer prison. The fire crackled, the warmth failing to reach the icy depths of his heart; Marcus tried not to hear the gunshots. They tore him from his sleep that night and every night since then. It had been a year since the night racism took his parents; their lives snuffed out by the cold indifference of two white cops. Officer Witling and Bebrigg; those names would forever live rent-free in his mind. They had responded to a domestic violence call, the reports say, but Marcus knew his parents never fought. The memory of their lifeless bodies, sprawled on the porch, haunted him every waking moment.

He had been alone ever since, bouncing from foster home to foster home, each a temporary haven before the inevitable rejection. No one wanted a bitter young man who detested everything in the world. The anger spread like venom throughout his entire body, and Marcus medicated it by fighting so much that homeschooling was his only remaining option. Marcus used to be outspoken and charismatic, but something had changed. The anger, the grief, the despair—they had coalesced into something else, something powerful.

The night was frigid, and the sky quickly packed with clouds like a rush-hour freeway. The grief twisted his stomach like wringing wet laundry, and he heard raindrops begin to cascade against the windows. The howling sound came from upstairs like wind rushing through a slightly opened window. The howling whistling was consistent, and Marcus could not drown it out as if I were inside his head. He followed the sound upstairs, searching for the open window as the whistling grew louder. There was a doorway that led to a terrace. Marcus stepped outside, and the rain began to pound on his shoulders, and his clothes felt like heavy hands pulling him down as they absorbed the torrent of rainfall. He was outside now, but he still heard the whistling. It had transformed into a singsong ah sound, and Marcus was determined to discover the source.

He saw a strange light pulsating from above the house, climbed on top of the railing, and leaped up to grab the edge of the awning in front of him. Marcus pulled himself up onto the roof and climbed upward toward the light. The wind whipped his hair as he stood on the rooftop of his latest foster home. The source of light was a small orb-shaped ball of light. It was pulsing and emitting the sound Marcus had followed. It wailed now but began to quiet down as Marcus walked toward it. The ball of light seemed to be calling and wanted him to touch it. He reached out, and the light crashed into his open palm and radiated through him. Marcus watched his entire body transform into light, and it went out. He had felt a surge of energy, a connection to the storm. He raised his hand, and a lightning bolt crackled down, striking the ground with a deafening roar.

He was different now. He was powerful. The power whispered promises of vengeance, making Witling and Bebrigg pay for their crimes. He could hunt them down, one by one, and make them suffer the same pain they had inflicted on his family.

But another voice spoke within him, a voice of reason and compassion. It reminded him of his parents, their love and kindness. They wouldn't want him to become a monster consumed by hatred. They would have him use his power for good, to protect the innocent, and to be a hero.

Marcus felt the tug of war inside him. The world had no love to show a young black orphan; it had no place for him. It threw him away repeatedly without batting an eye. He had every right to be angry and to seek revenge. But he also had the potential to be something more, to make a difference in a world that desperately needed change.

Marcus made his way back down the roof. The raindrops steamed as they touched his skin. He effortlessly swung himself from the awning onto the terrace and stepped inside. The steam continued to swirl around him as he walked. He looked around the inside of the house; the house was enormous, but he was aware that he was somehow too big for it now. He made his way back to the living room and the fireplace. The flames danced, and Marcus could feel them move, their warmth finally reaching him. Marcus reached out his hand again, closing it in front of the fireplace, and the flames disappeared. He opened his palm, and the fire danced in his hand. He stared at it, understanding its power, feeling it as his own. He closed his hand again, and the fire was gone. He knew what he had to do.

The next morning, Marcus left the foster home with a newfound determination. He would train, hone his abilities, and use them to protect those who couldn't defend themselves. He would be the protector his parents deserved. He would never let hatred consume another life or break another family.

The path ahead would be complex, fraught with danger and prejudice. But Marcus was no longer alone. He had his power, courage, and his parents' memory to guide him. He was ready to face the world, not as a victim, but as something else. The word hero didn't feel right to him; he wanted to be justice, even if that justice was ugly and dark. Marcus understood that some evil would never be vanquished with old-fashioned ideals of heroism. He wanted to be a real-time solution to real-life problems. He had not decided whether he would be a deterrent or a consequence. The only thing that Marcus was sure of, now, was that no one else would ever feel the despair that nearly destroyed him, and he would perfect his power to become a relief for the oppressed everywhere.

Conflicted

Martin Murphy

The sunlight peeped through the half-closed bamboo blinds, displaying a crescent on Davina's closed eyes. She acknowledged its wake-up call by slowly opening her eyes, and then she exhaled. Still exhausted from a night of intense pleasure, she greeted the day conflicted and torn. She lay there for what felt like hours. Her mind was fully engaged. Thoughts fired, one after another, like a newly lit pack of firecrackers popping off. She thought to herself, 'Oh God, how am I going to do this?' Davinia had never considered the consequences of her past decisions until now, and God was never part of that equation. He wasn't part of her current struggle either, but in complete exacerbation, she dug deep to find a solution to her problem. It felt like now or never.

She felt the bed move, then heard the voice she'd come to love, "Honey, are you okay?" It was Nicolas, the man responsible for her conflicted disposition. He reached over and lightly touched the small of her back, ran his thumb down her side, and gently squeezed in so she'd know he was there for her without saying a word.

She responded, "Oh, Yeah, I'm, I'm good honey, it's nothing. I'm just taking my time sliding out of bed this morning." That was her usual response when thoughts of her past flooded her mind. She was flooded with the threat of her joy being destroyed and losing the love that had grown with Nicolas. She was a master at using diversionary tactics. Using them helped mask the dark past she'd so skillfully hidden for the past three years. 'He deserves to know,' she toiled. The mental anguish burst at the seams of her mind, screaming to be released.

Nicolas was the first man, since her childhood, whom Davinia felt relaxed with. She had long pursued that perfect peace and found it with him. She experienced a sense of vulnerability, and the thought of losing it terrified her. She slid closer to the edge of the bed, feet barely touching the floor, head slightly lowered, and eyes closed. Her lips twitched and puckered as the conflicting memories poured in.

He interrupted her thoughts, "Babe, you sure you're good?" He continued to press. "I got you if you…"

Davinia interrupted with a few quick nods. "Yeah, I'm, uhm, I'm good." The short moments of silence that followed were deafening.

"Okay, well, you wanna hop up and head down to the café? I'm starving and I think they open at 8." He raised his head, grabbed the phone, and confirmed the time. "It's 9:30, you hungry?"

Davinia didn't respond right away. She slid off the side of the bed, planted her feet firmly on the floor, and without turning around spoke with an unperceived quiver in her voice, "Uhm, yeah, that sounds good." Then she headed toward the bathroom, avoiding direct eye contact. She didn't want Nicolas to see her tear-filled eyes because she knew he would press for answers. Answers, not because he felt she was hiding something, but because of his love and admiration for her. She struggled with demons of old. She'd lost count of the number of men she'd "expired" over the years, and she'd long forgotten the feel of a soft and gentle touch. Her appearance never betrayed her past: a cunning, lethal death-dealer for hire. Bored and thirsty for something more after a 15-year stint as a decorated Navy Seal and Army Ranger, she was lured into the life of an unforgiving mercenary for hire with global reach.

There she stood, in the bathroom, door locked and water running in an unplugged tub, to cover the sound of her gentle sob. 'What am I gonna do? Today could be the day I lose it all!' She thought as she stared into the mirror. A stunningly beautiful black widow of sorts. Capable of playing the tender-loving woman in need of a man's protection or easily ending their life. She was juxtaposed. She hated and loved what she saw in the mirror. The thought of exposing her dark past was unbearable. Especially with the man she never dreamed she'd come to love. She loved that she could completely let her hair down with Nicolas. She'd been as transparent as possible, without sharing her deepest disturbing secrets. Secrets she felt the need to bury for the embrace of a new love and passion. She yearned to live a long, abundant life with Nicolas. She heard the handle of the door being touched; three knocks followed.

"D, I need to use it. Why you lock the door???"

What's more important?

"You don't have to keep thanking me," Tori insisted. "I'm sure you'd do the same if I needed something. I was shocked you called. It's not like we've really talked in years, outside of sharing a few reels."

"I hate asking people for anything. Everyone's quick to say, 'Let me know if you need anything' but switch their phones on 'Do Not Disturb' if they even THINK you're about to ask for a favor." Keith replied.

"I understand," she responded. "I'm just glad you called. Feel free to stay as long as you want." She reassured him. "You see it's just me and Roscoe, and as much as I love my baby, it's great having an actual human here."

"Three days is more than enough to clear my mind." He told her. "I'll be out of your hair by tomorrow. Had I known I was gonna have an interview for this evening, I would've left last night." The stress of losing his job while the bills continued to amass at an alarming rate, became more and more daunting with each friendly reminder from his collectors.

"Everything happens for a reason," she smiled. "Use my office space upstairs for your Zoom call. I want you to be as comfortable and ready as possible. I'll be back in about an hour."

"I should be done by then." He assumed.

"Take your time." She replied. "Don't rush your greatness. They need to know they're getting the best when they get you." Her schoolgirl fondness for him, since the tenth grade, was now full-blown enamoredness. As a senior, he'd paid her no mind. Over the years he'd been oblivious to her comments under his post and the videos with hidden messages that landed in his DM.

"Remind me to use you as a reference in the future." They laughed, then she opened the door to the garage and backed out in her Lexus RZ. Neither her accomplishments nor extra-curricular support from afar were ever enough to get his full attention. He still viewed her as Lil T. She feared she'd forever be stranded in the purgatory of friend zones. When the garage door came to a close, sudden fear arose. He paced back and forth, clicking his pen. He went up and down the stairs repeatedly. He looked in the mirror, reciting possible answers to interview questions. He tried to calm his breathing and subside the rapid heart rate. He couldn't recall the last time he had an interview that mattered. You can be a confident candidate when you're currently employed: more of a leisure interview with minimal effort. It's a bit more tense when your livelihood's on the line. Eventually, he gave in and made his way to his vehicle, rambling both hands through the glove compartment and console. It had to be in there somewhere. He just needed a few puffs to ease the tension. He fumbled around for minutes. Failure to find it intensified the strain on his body. Maybe a few minutes in the sun would pacify his mental pain. A little vitamin D and conscious breathing to help refocus. He activated the garage opener by the door. The light disposed of the darkness, inspiring an instant smile. Three minutes would be all he needed. With composure gained and doubt diminished, he headed inside to be early for the Zoom. Before the garage could get halfway down, Roscoe dashed from under the car as if he'd been waiting for the perfect moment to play outside. Keith's pupils dilated and hysteria ensued when Roscoe took a left and ran past the mailbox.

"FUCK MY ENTIRE LIFE!" The neighbors were sure to hear his anguish. Anyone following Tori on social media could testify how she adored that dog, and now the guest of honor had to make a decision: what's more important, retrieving Roscoe or getting his life back on track? "I mean surely he'd find his way back home before Lil T returned. But what if he didn't? What if he got dognapped or worse? He'd be despised and ridiculed. Painted as the man who hated precious pets and couldn't be trusted alone in your house." Those thoughts, along with a few others, prompted him to make haste for the fury fleer. He hightailed it out of the garage and made the same left that Roscoe did. Unfortunately, his turn wasn't as graceful. His slick bottoms didn't mesh as well as Roscoe's paws with the pavement. "SPLAT!" His sideways fall was hard and loud. The concrete kept some of his dress shirt and slacks. He rolled over and popped up, hoping no one had seen or recorded the incident. Tori's security cam had indeed captured the humorous moment. The adrenaline masked most of the pain. He'd bear the brunt of it later that night. "ROSCOE!!" He called out several times. His phone vibrated. It was 15 minutes before his interview. He spent five more minutes combing the neighborhood, then his phone vibrated again. He looked at it for a while, then answered just before the voicemail took over.

"Hey!" Tori beamed with joy. "You logged in and ready?"

"Ugh, just about."

"Good!" She was pleased. "If you think Roscoe will be too loud, you can put him in one of the rooms downstairs."

"So far, I haven't heard a peep from him." He looked around, hoping to spot or hear something. "Is he much of an outside dog? If so, I can take him for a walk when I'm done. Anywhere he likes to go in particular?"

"No, not really. He just loves the outside in general. If you do take him out, keep his leash on. He doesn't know how to act without it."

"Hmm, that's good to know. I'll be sure to keep that in mind. Wouldn't wanna lose your baby."

"No, that wouldn't be good. Not at all."

"Umm, can I be honest with you?" With time ticking, he was running out of options.

"Always!"

"Roscoe got…" he stopped when he saw a lifesaving neighbor guiding Roscoe towards the house."

"He got what?" She wondered.

"He got into some trash I left out. Nothing serious. If I run out of time, I'll get the rest up after the call."

"Oh yeah, he can be a bit mischievous at times. It's not a big deal. Focus on getting the job, so we can celebrate before you leave."

Midway through the interview

Lead Interviewer: "Can you recall a time when you had to make a tough decision under pressure, and if so, how'd you handle it?

Happy as ever after this

"Today's the big day!" Anthony walked around the corner and into the room. He was known for making a conspicuous entrance.

"ANT!" Orlando greeted him with some dap and a hug. He hadn't seen his cousin in almost three years. "You looking sharp as a vaccine needle. If I didn't know any better, I'd think you were the one getting married."

"What, these old threads?" Anthony had always been a walking clothing store mannequin. He did whatever he had to do, to stay in the latest designs.

"It's good seeing you." Orlando introduced him to his groom party, and they chatted a little while. "We'll have to really make time to catch up after me and the wife get back from vacation."

"No doubt," Anthony replied. "I'm proud of you. Now let me go see what friends of the bride I can get friendly with." They shared another laugh. "I'll get with you at the reception." They embraced again, then Ant went to see what he could see. Not too long after that, Pastor Lewis came to speak with Orlando.

"Knock knock," they were always delighted to see him. "I hope you gentlemen are acting in accordance with the word."

"As best as we can Pastor," Orlando acted as the group's spokesperson. After Pastor Lewis exchanged pleasantries with the others, he and O started a one-on-one conversation.

"I want to thank you again, for all you've done and for allowing us to use your facilities."

Orlando was the thankful type. He made sure there was no uncertainty about his gratefulness.

"You know you don't have to thank me, son. Your faithful service over these years has helped us grow and led to many blessings. Be sure to share my gratitude with your father, as well." He was referring to his stepdad. Pastor had never met O's biological father, though he and his stepdad had a swell relationship.

"I spoke with him earlier today, and the respect is mutual. Although he was unable to make it, his brothers are here for support."

"Ahhh yes, it's nothing like a strong, supportive family in the house on your big day. I'm sure everything will go well; I'll see you and your queen to be at the altar." He patted O on his shoulder, nodded his head, and went back to his office."

The Bridal Party

"Are you sure about this?" Cynthia asked. "It's not too late to change your mind. Once you say, 'I do,' and get in that limousine, ain't no U-turns."

"I have nothing to lose and everything to gain. This is gonna be the best day of my life!" Brandy hoped her confident reply would ease her best friend's nerves.

"Aiight, just double checking," she wasn't going to bring it up again. "You know I got your back, no matter what, like a masseuse." Cynthia and Brandy had been friends since B.C. (Before Classrooms) They went to the same daycare and their parents stayed on the same street. If you looked up inseparable on the web, you just might find their picture. Brandy even stayed with

Cynthia's family for a few months, when her parents were having irreconcilable differences, that led to their divorce.

"We're family," Brandy assured her. "The only thing that's changing, is my last name and the numbers in my bank account."

Her bridal party applauded that statement and replied in unison, "YES, girl, that's what we talk'n bout!"

"Ladies, it's time to slay," the photographer gathered them up, so they could take the pre-wedding photos. The reception was at a different location, and Brandy didn't want to risk losing anyone en route.

The Peanut Gallery

"She looks so pretty up there," Marcie pointed out.

"I would hope so, with all that makeup she has caked on," Lucy retorted. "I was about to start calling her Brandy Crocker."

"Stop it."

"I'm serious," although, clearly she was being facetious. Lucy was the type that knew, or so she thought, everyone's business, what was best for them, and what they needed to do better. "She definitely settled."

"Why you say that?" Marcie asked.

"He doesn't even have a real job. I heard the church had to supply what they needed."

"But he's in school to be a doctor or something like that, right?"

"Don't get me to lying," not that Lucy had a problem lying. "I heard he be on campus socializing more than he's in class.

"Maybe that's a good trait for a doctor: being friendly."

"Maybe it's a red flag for a husband."

Marcie giggled, "I can't argue with that one," she conceded.

"Not to mention, she barely knows him," Lucy was only saying what most people were thinking.

"They say when you know, you know."

"Well, I may not know a lot, but I know that ain't half the time it takes to get to know someone you're finna to marry," Lucy replied.

"Where'd they meet, anyway?" Marcie inquired.

"They said, at a church function."

"Church function?"

"Yeah, they were both in some sort of 'young adults dealing with divorced parents' trauma' therapy group, or something like that."

"Word?"

"Yep. She posted some of those 'how it started vs. how it's going' photos on social media. Look," She showed Macie her phone. "They had a bonfire, trail ride, and a bunch of other backwoods events."

"I see they even played games," Marcie motioned to a photo of Brandy holding a horseshoe, with a smile big enough to change Eeyore's mood. "He might just be the one," she added. "I don't think a game of horseshoes or s'mores can make anyone THAT happy."

"Exactly! Faking for the gram," Lucy shook her head in disapproval.

It's go time!

"I now pronounce you husband and wife," Pastor Lewis made it official. "You may now kiss the bride." Cheers and tears flowed from different family, friends, and loved ones. The photographer captured the moments before they passed by, and the newlyweds made their way to their limo. The bride threw her bouquet through the falling rice, waved goodbye, and then got in the decorated ride.

"Oh, my GOODNESS!" Brandy shouted. "Can you believe we did this?"

"It's still sinking in," O said, as he looked out the window at their police escort.

"I know right, who would've thought!? I can't wait to get to the room and celebrate."

"Honestly, it kept crossing my mind while we were face to face," O added. "I almost told Pastor Lewis, 'Hurry up, so we can get to the good stuff," the new couple laughed without conviction. It was about a forty-five-minute drive, unless traffic was dense, from the church to their hotel. Not that they had to worry about traffic, with "CHiPs" leading the way.

When they arrived at the five-star resort, valet greeted them with a smile and took care of their luggage. "We'll be staying in the honeymoon suite," Orlando was grinning like the Cheshire Cat when he said it. They thanked the officers for getting them there without incident and made their way up to the temporary, amorous abode. They were overwhelmed by applause and congratulations from the various strangers they passed on their way up. When they made it to the room, Orlando knocked on the door instead of using his room card.

Jackpot

"Get in here!!!" Carlos pulled his stepson inside and hugged him like he'd hit the winning home run in the World Series. "What did I tell you? What did I tell you?!"

"That I had nothing to worry about," O admitted. "You were right, as usual." Carlos was known for "playing" chess, not checkers. He strategized and thought eight to ten moves ahead. He'd foreseen this day happening, way back, when Orlando first joined the church. Carlos and Lewis were friends, long before "pastor" was attached to his name, which made it a logical decision for him to reach out to Carlos when the budget books became invariably in the red.

"I can't believe the police gave us an escort here!" Brandy was still in disbelief.

"Not only that, but they helped me load ALL the bags in the ride. I just knew one of 'em was gonna bust open or they ask to see inside," O was known for overthinking. "If they only knew what they aided us with today, they'd blow a slew gasket."

"This was the biggest transport of product we've done in YEARS," Carlos was triumphant. "We're almost to the point where we can stop using the church as our major storage unit and move on to even greater things."

"Like only legal ventures?" O asked, hoping for a yes.

"Ahhh yes my son," with one hand on O's arm and the other on the left side of his face he continued, "Always thinking of how we can get out of the game for good and you open up your practice."

"Practice? With the money we'll make off of today's move, he can open hospitals," the bride shared her two cents.

"Either way it's legal, and I'll sleep better at night."

"With this type of money, you can buy sleep," nothing could rid Carlos' mind of what they'd just accomplished. "I know you have to get down to the ballroom soon, and I must prepare for the buyers on the way, but let's start the fiesta here." He motioned for one of his servants to bring the drink tray over. "A toast to the bride and groom." They lifted their glasses. "May you live happy as ever after this!"

They Choosing

DAMN! Something TOLD me to leave her at home. Then again, had I rolled solo it would've been BONE-dry. But that's beside the point. They crawling round here like it's infested and I'm the Orkin man: ready to spray until they sprawled out shaking with shattered nerves. I definitely would've left with SOMETHING. I gotta think of a master plan. I've been in tighter situations and still came through in the ninth inning.

"What's wrong? Something on your mind?

Here she go with that diva discernment. Woman intuition on weed. Feminine focus. Dionne Warwick psychic hotline head.

"Hellooo."

I can't even get a minute to reply, yet it takes her 85 minutes to get ready. "I'm straight. Was just thinking about that 15-leg parlay Jayson Tatum cost me. If it wasn't for him, we'd be butt naked on a beach in Maui, making love on the shore, with nothing but leis around our necks, looking up at the stars while the soft waves splash your ass."

"Sounds great, dear. In the meantime, let's enjoy our present reality until me and that damp dream can come true."

I'd be enjoying it if you weren't raining on my potential new pussy parade. All this new booty, blocked by my current beauty. This can't be life. "Of course, love. I wouldn't wanna be vibing anywhere else, except maybe in Maui, but here with you" and the rest of these half-dressed bad bouncing batches. Let's see if I can create a little space in this place. All I need is a little daylight: Steph Curry don't miss in the clutch. Hands down, man down. Drop your guard and I'm scoring. "You want another drink or anything?"

"No, I'm fine. Thank you."
Oh, TONIGHT you're fine. Any other time you'd be requesting your third or fourth drink by now. Ain't that bout a flip. She can sense the eyes on me. Probably the main reason she closer than rush hour traffic. All touchy-feely like, "Yeah this me."

"Don't forget I can't be out late."
We can leave right now. Just gimmie the word. The sooner I get you up outta here, the faster I can double back and clean up like housekeeping. "I understand, boo. We can make up for lost time and have an all-nighter tomorrow." When I

get back, I plan to find 'Ms. Right' in here and move her panty line to the left to the left. I'ma hit that box with everything that I own til she runs outta breath. Mmmmmm.

"I'm going to the bathroom."

Take all the time you need. I'm bout to plant some seeds that I can sprinkle later. "Cool. I'm a grab a last drink before we head out." Here we go. I'm on the clock like nine to five. Let me set my watch like the Equalizer. Denzel ain't got $#!+ on ME. They be at the bar, just WAITING for a G like me to make their day. Clint Eastwood would be proud. Yes SURRRRRR. I'll be back for you, you, you, you, and maybe even you."

"Scuse me. Is that your girl, you sitting with over there?"

Look at this. She couldn't WAIT til my lady left the table to shoot her shot. All slick and subtle with her hand on my back. What she don't know is I BEEN peeped her and her girlfriend pointing and smiling my way. I stay two steps ahead like the line leader. "It depends, who wants to know?"

"Well, my friend sent me over to ask…" Preciate it, but I got it from here. I love a direct woman who knows what she wants and the perfect time to go for it. I'd let you finish but I'm pressed for time so let me guide you to the jackpot, "I knew I saw you both looking my way."

"Why yes. Yes, we were."
How could you not? The drip is too saucy like twice wet wings. "I'm a be honest. We're together but it's not that serious. I'm actually

bout to take her home. You have a gorgeous smile, by the way. Is your friend shy or playing things safe with the scout team?"

"She can be a little coy until you get to know her. Once she feels you out, she'll open up."

I bet she will. I'm something like a pro magician. Nice with the hands, words, and entertainment, but no tricking: open sesame! Let's show begin. I'm built for an encore. Do you want more?

"Did your fine friend give you the authority to share her contact information?"

"No doubt. She didn't send me for play-play."

SEE! THAT'S what I'm talking about! I wish more women were bout their business. Life's too short for playing 21 questions or guessing games.

Get to it, so you can put your back into it. "I like her already."

"There's a minor but major caveat, though."
Isn't it always, sweetheart? Whether it's upfront or pops out later like a vintage Jack-in-the-box from a few turns: surprise, surprise... "Oh yeah? And what's that?

"We were actually looking at your date. She'd like you to give her number to your girl if you don't mind. I mean, since it's not that serious and all, why not?"
Why not? Why not?? Why don't I KNOT your head up just for disrespecting ME!? How you gone halla at my girl -not just 'in front of me'- using me as the messenger pigeon? I ain't Will Smith (Spies in Disguise). I am LEGEND. You better put some respect on my name like Byron

Williams. Can't believe she had the gall to propose something so indecent as if I'm Woody Harrelson. But I digress. "I'm sure she'd be flattered, love, but my pretty Nicki don't get down with the gowns. At least not solo. I might can convince her, when the time is right, to tag team your friend, or maybe we can make it a title match with the four of us, but that about it."

"Thanks, but that's ok. We'll catch her another day."

You lucky you ain't catch these hands. I'm tryna to be civil but I'm close to the edge. Keep on pushing and see what happens, ya dirty deceiving damsel; confused concubine; janky Jezebel; heartless hooker; harlot in heat. "Best wishes to you as well." Let me get back to my good and wholesome woman before I'm corrupted by these courtesans.

Pretty Dress

Writers Refuge

Ashley ran into the yard of the vacant flat, searching for a hiding place. Any place was better than being exposed. The thought of being caught made the hairs on her neck stand up. She had seen those raggedy teeth peep from behind that evil grin earlier and it made her shudder in fear at the thought of seeing them again, but the prickling sensation on her neck forced her to look over her shoulder, hoping to avoid that grisly view. She wasn't certain if she'd placed a safe distance between her and what she thought to be certain death, but with footsteps getting closer, she had to make a split decision.

Would it be the dilapidated, lifeless building which was surely a death trap, or a thicket of bushes to hide in? She dove behind the bushes. She realized the rapid, heavy breathing and pounding heart wouldn't help in concealing her location. Ashley gripped the hem of her dress with one hand, and with her precious blanket attempted to trap any noise from escaping. Tears rolled down her cheeks and she closed her eyes, hoping the nightmare would end as he walked past the yard.

She had an impulse to raise her head and glance for his whereabouts, but the fear of being discovered was overwhelming. Ashely concentrated on the sound of his approach. She could tell from his gait, as he dragged one foot on the ground. 'Why can't I outrun this limping man,' she thought. She waited, for what seemed like an eternity, for the right moment to dart from the bushes. Once content with the absence of moving sounds, she opened her eyes and peeked through the shrubbery. Although she didn't see anything, there was still that eerie tingle on her neck. She then looked up and there he was, two feet above her. She screamed and tried to get up but lost her footing and fell backward. His black trench coat blended into the night. He appeared to be floating when he reached over the bushes and nearly grabbed her arm but grabbed her blanket instead. Ashley fought to get away without losing her grip on the beloved blanket. She was rarely seen without it. It had brought her comfort and peace ever since she was a toddler. It was the only thing she had of her twin since he tragically passed.

Saliva and mucus dripped down on her face as his raspy voice slurred, "Come herrre Pretty Dresssss; look at you now. Gett'n dat dress all dirtied up. It's ok, you're home now." In a panic, Ashley got up and ran into the abandoned building. There were no doors or windows to stop him from following her, and that's exactly what he did. She ran down a dark hallway, into the doorless kitchen, and straight to the back door. Desperate and flush with adrenaline, Ashley tried to open the door but to no avail. She glared around, looking for her pursuer. The deafening silence was agonizing. She squinted through the dim light provided by a lamp post from the alley which pierced through a filthy shattered window. She noticed down the hall a set of stairs, one leading down to deeper darkness and one leading upward, but she wanted out.

Then she heard him, his palms gripped both sides of the doorless frame and he poked his head into the house listening for movement. That evil-slurred growl calmly called out, "Pretty Dress." He pulled himself through the entrance, dragging his leg over the threshold of the rotten front doorway. Here he was, enjoying his taunt. "Oh, Pretty Dress, why do you run?" That innocent tone morphed into an evil snarl. "As if you could get away."

Ashley's startled yelp gave away her location. Amused at her trapped situation he laughed, "Ahhh, now you see why my back door stays locked, I see you've found the kitchen. Tell me Pretty Dress, are you hungry" I surely am?" He was never satisfied.

Her faint defeated whimper marked her devastation. She slid along the wall, reaching for anything she could find, stumbling her way through the broken darkness until she found another knob. He made his way down the entrance hallway with haste. "What do you want to eat, Petty Dress?" The sound of chomping teeth struck more fear into her. He continued, "I sure know what I'd like to sink my teeth in." Ashley moved through the tenebrous decayed shell of a room with wariness. For stability, she gripped onto what she thought was a knob until it moved.

After Ashley stumbled to the nasty floor, she began to crawl and felt her way through the house. All of a sudden, the filth began to squirm under her hands and knees. Small creepy crawlers slithered and clambered up her limbs. She could feel the vermin tickling her skin. She wanted nothing more than to escape. Before she could, she felt a cold bony hand take hold of her lower leg, she cried out, "Please, somebody! Help me, please! He's trying to…" Her screams for help were disrupted as he yanked at her leg and caused her face to hit the floor. Insects were tangled in her hair and sprawled across her face. She kicked and fought until her foot struck the side of his face. Her moment to escape was met with heavy coarse intonation, "Oh Pretty Dress. There is NO escape. Look at what you have done to that pretty dress."

Ashley ran to the exit and with vigorous motions, attempted to remove the insects from her hair and body. She ran out of the house, across the yard, scurried down the block, and pleaded for help. There was no one around to help. The only thing she saw was a building with lights at the end of the block. How had she missed it? She heard him yell, "Pretty Dress!

You are mine!" The joy of safety and the release of stress gave her hope amidst his callings. The bumps started to rise on her skin again. She took a quick glimpse over her shoulder and there he was, dragging his foot. He was relentless and persistent, coming for her even though she reached refuge.

She turned, picked up the pace, and reached the building just in time. She dashed into the building and squinted from the bright lights. She saw a police officer, who stood with EMTs. She pleaded, "Help! He's after me!" There was no response. "HELP ME!!" she continued. Still no reply. Ashley, confused and frustrated, began to wonder why no one responded to her pleas. She fumed in silence, then turned and noticed her. A woman who sat next to the EMTs with her face buried in her hands was crying inconsolably. Her sobs tugged at the strings of Ashley's heart. There was a strong connection, but Ashley didn't know why. Without realizing it, Ashley walked towards the woman. With every step, the scene became clear. Flashing lights, shattered glass, her blood-stained blanket, random metal shards, yellow tape, and a motionless body which the lady cried over. "Not my other baby."

Ashley began to feel light-headed and detached from her reality. Her heart stopped when she recognized that the woman with the bloody face, wailing over the body, was her mother and the body was, 'ME!? How could this be?' Ashley pondered in disbelief as she watched her lifeless body lay out on the pavement.

"CLEAR!" The EMT used the AED to revive Ashley again.

Ashley felt that familiar prickle race over her body once more, her extremities stiffened, and went limp again as the charge faded.

"We have no pulse," realizing the inevitable, the EMT stopped. "Let's get her to the trauma unit. Don't stop trying to get a heartbeat, team."

The officer looked over at the other car involved in the accident, "Your night just went from bad to worse, buddy." The officer barked while he walked towards the man in the black trench coat. "Turn around," the officer pulled out his cuffs. The man in the trench coat clambered to his feet, drug his broken leg, and incoherently complained of pain.

"Such a pretty dress," he continued to repeat what he had rambled since they pulled him from his smashed vehicle in between sobs. "Is she ok?" he half hissed.

With disgust the officer replied, "You should have thought about that before you got behind the wheel, drunk."

The Reporter's Missing Story

Dominic Murphy

Oh, man! Did you guys see what just happened to Denise? "That's what the mean little boy yelled across the playground laughing and pointing at me as I lay beside the monkey bars disoriented. One of the little girls jumped from the slide laughing and screamed 'What just happened? Why did she fall like that?' This was the first time it happened to me, that I'm told, but I don't remember anything myself. The teacher told Rufus… Or… or my father, I guess. Fresh after the seizure, I was acting lost and lethargic. But as I said, I don't remember anything about that seizure. I do remember, however, waking up at a doctor's office on the floor looking up at the ceiling. I wanted to get up but had no real control over my muscles and limited control over my thoughts. I lay there on my back motionless for what seemed like an eternity. The only movement was my eyes shifting back and forth, trying to figure out my surroundings. I heard the voices, but none were familiar. The crazy part is… This was a Saturday morning, and we were usually in church… The disturbing part is… The last thing I remembered before waking up in the doctor's office, was going to school the Tuesday before the seizure on the playground happened."

Her Psychiatrist, Dr. Yastina Forleston, usually responded with a head nod and hmm, but now and then she would say, "OK!' and, "I see!"

Denise continued, "So from that moment until I woke up in the doctor's office, do not exist in my memory bank. That's how it's always been. That qualifies as crazy and disturbing don't you think?"

The doctor responded, "I'm sure, at the time, that was disturbing." She flipped through her book and looked over a few notes then asked, 'How long have you been having these seizures and how frequent are they now?"

"I've had seizures as far back as… uhm… hmmm," Denise gazed off into the distance and pondered. "Maybe about seven… or maybe even eight from what I can recall… And I only have vague memories of half of those. The other half someone usually tells me about, but whenever I wake up, I'm usually four days behind, yet never behind in classwork, chores, work assignments, or anything like that. The only thing I lose… is time."

"Interesting!" Dr. Forleston jotted in her notebook. She sat her notes to the side, at this moment in the session. "Ok Denise, I'm going to have you try something for me." She then pulled out a marker and sketchbook. "I want you to put down the first thing that comes to mind when I say a word."

Denise smiled and a little excitement peaked in her voice, "Oh. OK! This is new."

Dr. Forleston seemed very intrigued by her statement, "Hmmm! So, you've never done this exercise before?" She looked up at Denise to observe her body language. Denise remained engaged and enthused when she shook her head 'no' but never uttered a word. She began to draw flowers and balloons in the corner on the open page of the sketchbook. As she wrote in her notes, the doctor was fixated on Denise's doodling. "OK, Denise! Let's begin." The doctor dived into the exercise with five or six words, then suddenly, Denise stopped and rapidly tapped the marker on the pad. It fell from her right hand and rolled to the floor. She smacked her lips together a few times and closed her eyes. The noticeably small twitch in her left wrist captured the doctor's attention. This occurred for less than fifteen seconds and when Denise came to, she reached up with the softest touch, rubbed her lips with her right hand, and leaned over to pick up the marker with her left hand.

It twitched one last time and then she recited, "That was close."

The doctor grew more entranced in her silence. She appeared to unveil a genuine expression that her concerns and questions were well thought out. She inhaled and exhaled deep and slow, then made eye contact and asked, "Close? Was that a seizure or almost a seizure?"

Denise smiled, but with a sedated tone and a just-above-whispering voice she responded, "Sometimes I can feel my…" She stopped and took a sharp breath in, "self-fading. But then my inner voice tells me, 'I got this, I got this.' And the seizure goes away. Sometimes I keep a garlic clove with me because when I get a taste of metal in my mouth, I sniff the garlic and it stops the seizure."

"Hmmm… OK!" The doctor wrote in her notes again, then asked, "So are you sure those aren't Partial-Onset Seizures? At least that's what it sounds like." Denise Shrugged her shoulders but never looked up because she was focused on the sketch pad.

Dr. Forleston softened her voice as she leaned in and asked, "Can you continue?"

Denise nodded yes, then paused, looked around the room, and began to nod yes again.

"OK, so you've answered all my questions." The doctor continued, "You've completed the exercise. But I'm not sure I believe that your story about your first seizure is your craziest and most disturbing or if it's just the memory of the moment the crazy disturbances began. Do you think it's possible to dig deeper and tell me about the craziest and most disturbing seizure you remember?"

With a brief reluctance, Denise looked away but decided to share a moment she still had partial details of. She dropped her head and with an eerie slowness, lifted her eyes. Once she made eye contact with the psychiatrist, she spoke slower and firmer than she had been speaking. "Well DOC, since you twisted my arm, maybe you can help me understand or unlock a mystery I have been struggling with for the past nine years." She wrote on the sketch pad before speaking again, "One Thursday I was supposed to be in school, but I woke up… In the bathroom at home." Denise broke eye contact and stared down at her fingers twirling the string from her hoodie around the marker. She then began writing without answering Dr. Forleston. She tensed up this time and twitched for less than five seconds.

The confused doctor nodded and asked, "Was that another Partial-Onset?"

Once again Denise nodded yes with a little more zeal and vibrancy.

Dr. Forleston, still waiting for Denise to finish, inquired, "Well, I'm sure there's more, if we're REALLY digging deeper, right?" The room once again went silent. "What is the mystery? What's so disturbing about this particular seizure when you woke up in the bathroom, Denise?"

Denise avoided eye contact, leaned back on the couch, looked up at the ceiling, and took a deep breath. She closed her eyes, blew the air from her lips, and began to tilt her head back down. At the end of her long breath, she locked eyes, leaned forward, and said, "I was standing in the mirror with dirt under my nails and dried blood on my hands." Denise stared at the doctor and the corners of her mouth crept up and she tried to hide behind the awkward smile she exhibited.

The consultation was close to wrapping up, but Dr. Forleston not only wanted to hear the disturbing story Denise started sharing, but she also wanted to give her closing review. The doctor explained, "There are only ten minutes left and I would like to hear the rest of this particular seizure before my closing review."

While the doctor was talking, Denise's phone rang, and she reached into her right pocket, but the phone was in her left pocket. Once she finally retrieved the phone and put it up to her right ear, she said, "Hello... And you are?" She put a finger up to request the doctor give her a second. But as soon as she got ready to speak on the phone again, she twitched and dropped the phone. She picked it up with her left hand this time and continued talking. Then, without completing the session, she walked out of the doctor's office.

The stunned doctor walked over to the table to clean up and prepare for the next patient and saw on the sketch pad the words, 'Tell her my story the way it's written *I was standing in the mirror with dirt under my nails and dried blood on my hands.*'

Innocent

Barry Tyson

The car engine hummed a low droning hypnotic
sound. The wheels bump bump bumped across
the gravel road like B2K fans, and Manyah
thought about the proceedings of the previous
hours. 'I graduated law school today!' She
celebrated in her head. Her lips curled slowly
outward and upward; the corners stretched
across her face like an upside-down umbrella.
'My dream has always been to become a
lawyer…a good one.' She added the stipulation
and nodded in approval as the thought pleased
her. She laughed as she recollected all the
YouTube videos she had posted as a child
mimicking her favorite law shows and mused at
the mock trials she had created in cinematic

fashion. Her fan views over the years continued to swell, as did her desire to make it all a reality. Her page had become quite popular, and she had been a top influencer for years. 'I can't believe I scheduled an interview today… no, I rocked an interview today.' She nodded again and pumped her fist in the air like she was in the front row at the best concert ever. This time, she said "Yeah" out loud as she admired her success. '28 and feeling great!' she gloated within herself. The interview she continued to beam about, was the reason she was driving on a gravel road. She was audacious enough to schedule an interview with Bellings and Fordge, one of the top law firms in the state, and Mr. Fordge himself agreed to meet with her. He understood the power of her celebrity status and admired it. He had been a long-time fan of her YouTube videos and had always hoped her path would cross his. The interview, if you would even call it that, was short. Mr. Fordge told her how much he adored her work, knew she would be a fine lawyer someday, and would be delighted to help. His law firm was opening a new firm with the idea of hiring all young and up-starting lawyers; he offered her the position of Managing Partner.

"If you accept, meet me at this address to celebrate later." Mr. Fordge smiled and leaned over his desk to hand her a paper with directions. Manyah hadn't realized how much she was trembling until she reached for the address. Her hand shook like turbulence on a cheap flight, and she blushed as she recalled the moment.

"In 20 feet, make a left turn on Orchard Lane." The navigation voiced directions and snapped her back to the present moment. She had never been this far into the woods before. She was never much of a nature gal. The road snaked this and that way. It was rough and untraveled. The sun was beginning to retreat behind the horizon, leaving streaks of amber across the sky and burnt orange waves of color spread above the trees. The road came to a clearing; on one side was a beautiful lake and a two-story cottage house. On the other side, the trees stood tall and majestic, lined perfectly alongside the road to the house. It was breathtaking. She was consumed by the beauty of it all and didn't notice the young deer that had stepped into the road. It was sudden, and she swerved to avoid it and slid off the gravel road into a tree. The deer startled and darted away back into the woods. Manyah was unsure how much time had passed before the car door was snatched open, but it felt instantaneous. Two prominent arms reached in and pulled her from the banged-up vehicle. She was disoriented and dizzy, but she knew muscles when she saw them, and these were definitely that. She followed the chiseled forearms upward and was surprised to find Mr. Fordge's face at the end of all that bulging sinew. She thought, 'I don't remember those at the interview.' She fell into his massive arms as he carried her towards the cottage. She rested her head on his chest and closed her eyes.

"No, no, sweetheart, you gotta stay awake. Concussion protocol or something like that."

Mr. Fordge smiled, and Manyah remembered feeling warm and cozy all over. He covered the distance between the car and the cottage as if he didn't have a young lady in his arms. The door was slightly ajar. He pushed it open with his foot and swept it closed behind them. He sat her down on the couch. "Remember, be comfortable, but no sleeping," he admonished, waving a giant finger at her as he disappeared down the hall. He reappeared with a warm towel and pressed it firmly against her forehead. It wasn't until that moment that she realized she was bleeding. Her eyes bulged, and Mr. Fordge quickly consoled her. "It's ok, just a tiny scratch. You're going to be fine." Something about his voice's softness made her believe him, and she calmed herself. "Is there someone you would like me to call?"

"No, my parents would send an entire rescue team," she paused to chuckle. "They are both masters of overreacting." She reached up to hold the towel and noticed her hand trembling again. This time, she wondered if the situation or the man was causing her involuntary tremors. Manyah set her hand on top of his as she stared at the contour of his chest through the tight silk shirt. It was mid-spring, but she was sure the weather was not why she was hot. Mr. Fordge slowly slid his hand free, and Manyah barely avoided drooling as he began to speak again.

"Other than needing a new headlight, the car should be fine, and I feel somewhat responsible. Please allow me to take care of it." He disappeared into the kitchen and came back with a bottle of water. Manyah accepted although she knew it would not quench the thirst she was currently experiencing. She crossed her legs, trying to subdue the throbbing that had begun between them. She bit her lower lip as she daydreamed about him carrying her upstairs to a bedroom. He was older and mature; she had always had a thing for older men. The butterflies in her stomach were doing something supernatural as her insides swirled in a manner she had never experienced before. She continued to fantasize as he examined her, making sure she was indeed injury-free. She inhaled as he leaned over her. His aroma was intoxicating. He peeled back the towel to examine her forehead. There, it stopped bleeding. It doesn't even look like it will scar. That beautiful face will be just fine."

Manyah sat up as he carried away the soiled towel and disappeared down the hall again. 'Wait... did he say beautiful? Is he... nah, he's not.' She debated whether Mr. Fordge was just being kind or flirting. Everything in her hoped it was the latter. She hadn't noticed how attractive he was earlier, but now she could not see how she had missed it. She was confident the butterflies would erupt from her abdomen and fly around the room at any moment. She stood up and paced in front of the couch. What was it her mother always said? 'Follow guts... no, instincts were trustworthy, or miss meals, not opportunities...' There was a myriad of elderly wisdom swirling in her mind; she had never felt like this about anyone so suddenly. She worried she was being childish and impetuous. But what if she wasn't? What if this could be more than infatuation? She was wrenching her hands together when Mr. Fordge reentered the room.

He discerned her unease and asked, "Is everything ok?" Before he could finish the question and she could talk herself out of it, she stepped into him and placed her lips softly against his. The adrenaline swelled within her, and her knees weakened, and he held her tightly. Time felt as if it had stopped entirely as she floated in his arms, lost in the moment as her lips massaged his.

Janae

Janise Williams

Janae Wilks was entering her last week of summer before starting her first year of College at Smith University. Smith University was the college that both of her parents attended. They met there many years ago. Both of her parents were white. They adopted Janae at three months old. She was 19 now and couldn't remember a year she hadn't wondered who her parents were and why they didn't want her. She was dark-skinned, beautiful, tall, and curvy. Her beautiful baby doll eyes were green as emeralds. Her pretty hair was long and thick. She kept her body toned. She loved and hated her features. Loving them was easy but because of those same attributes, the white girls at the school secretly, and sometimes openly, despised her. She joined groups, clubs, and cheer teams to fit in, but none of it worked. Nothing stopped the consistent tyranny from the jealous girls. Janae's parents showed her nurturing and affectionate love anytime anyone made her feel like she wasn't welcome or didn't matter. Their words of care and comfort momentarily helped her feel superior, but she struggled to keep her head up daily. Smith University was a predominately white college. It was her parent's dream for her. She desired to attend Spelman College. She longed to be around people who looked like her and experience something different. She shared those sentiments with her parents, but if their money had anything to do with her tuition, then Smith University it.

"Today's the day." Janae encouraged herself. She got up at 5:00 am. Her nerves wouldn't allow her to sleep well. She hoped her morning run would relieve some of her anxiety. She ran a full sprint. As she ran through the neighborhood, she couldn't help but reminisce about her childhood as the wind whistled through her ponytail. She thought about the new opportunities that college could bring. She knew every inch of that neighborhood. She was itching to leave the small town and enjoy something new. When she reached the corner of her block, she noticed something new and unpromising. The unusual sight made the hairs on her neck stand up: a ragged, gray SUV on the corner where there weren't any houses. The front grill was missing, and the bumper sagged as if it were pondering falling off at any moment. The windows were dark from a limousine-type tint. She could barely make out the silhouette of the lone occupant. That SUV didn't belong there. She crept to the other side of the street, hoping to avoid the occupant of the vehicle. Before she could create a suitable space, she heard the car door open and slam behind her. Everything in her screamed "RUN!" But before her feet could obey, someone pushed her down from behind. At first glance, she noticed that this girl looked exactly like her. She wiped her eyes and shook her head.

"No, you're seeing right." The girl said. She waved a knife in Janae's face.

"But how?" Janae said.

"I'm the sister that didn't get away." She answered. "Mom chose to give you up. She said couldn't handle twins. YOU got lucky. She should've done me a favor and gave me up too. But no! I had the pleasure of living with that drunk bitch! She hit me every chance she got. She hated that I reminded her of you and Dad." She rambled on, half-talking to herself. Her eyes were wild and crazed. Spit flew from her mouth as she talked. "But you… you got to live the good life. All up in the hills with the rich white folks. ME? I was a fucking punching bag!"

Janae was stunned. She struggled to process the words and the fact that a girl she never knew, with the same face and shape, was yelling at her while flaunting a knife. The creepy twilight version of her continued to vent, "Your mom was pathetic drunk. One night she told me about the precious baby she gave away. I did my research. I been watching you ever since." As she jabbered, the blade continued to make its way near Janae's skull.

"I didn't know," Janae spoke softly. She carefully pleaded with her crazed twin, trying not to startle or agitate her. As the girl continued to rant, she flung the knife around like a toy. Janae envisioned an ear being severed or an eye lost with each swipe. "Please, if we're sisters, let me make things right. Come home with me. We can figure this out." Janae tried to slowly scoot away, but her deranged assailant pounced on her and grabbed her ponytail.

"Oh, you think I'm dumb? You ain't slick! You're a liar just like your mom WAS." Janae's blood ran cold. Her dreams of one day meeting her mother were instantly demolished. "And to think, I almost let you go off to college…. You were gonna leave me again…. I… I… I was supposed to be right there with you. YOU WILL NEVER SEE IT!!!" Without warning, Janae felt a sharp, horrible pain as her twin repeatedly bludgeoned her stomach and her clothes turned red. She always wanted someone to feel connected to; to know her family and belong with her own. Her desire turned to disaster as she watched her life slowly seep from the holes in her abdomen. Drenched in blood, she was too shocked to scream. She tried to grab her sister's hands, but her body went limp. She watched in horror as the sister she always wanted slid the knife across her throat, ending the sisterhood she craved her entire life.

Late for no reason

"AW, SHIT!!" Davion smashed his fist into the bed after realizing the time on his cell phone. He threw off the covers as if they were trying to violate him. The expletives continued as he swung his feet to the side of the bed, bypassed his house shoes, and hurried towards his daughter's room. He bumped into the wall in the hallway but kept his balance and refocused like a pro running back playing for a contract. Inevitably it'd leave a bruise on his shoulder and a dent in the drywall. Right before the opportunity to wake her, he stepped on a toy, releasing a sound typically reserved for someone being slammed, blindsided, or hit in the face with a foul ball. He took the time he didn't have to regain his fatherly bearing, not wanting his only child to witness her Superhero moaning like an average Joe. No father in his right mind wants his children to lose that reverence, deserved or not, for him. Even if it's fiction.

"Wake up, wake up, wake up…" He pulled back her unicorn comforter, as not to startle but to encourage the opening of her eyes. She was still as a statue. He exhaled for five seconds, "I should've put her to sleep earlier" while shaking his head. He lifted her lifeless body and kissed her, smacking his lips as loudly as possible. Her eyes opened like a newborn for the first time, trying to make sense of her surroundings. You would've thought she finally met a long-time idol the way her eyes sparkled, and smile grew. For a moment he forgot they were late, enthralled by her unconditional love, awe, and innocence. She hugged him like she'd never see him again. Back focused on the crisis at hand, he carried her into the bathroom. "Can you brush your teeth while Daddy gets your clothes?" She gave the look and nod of approval, then positioned her stepping stool near the sink, while he turned the water handle and lined her tiny toothbrush with colorful fruity paste. Had he foreseen the unpunctual predicament they'd be in, he would've picked her fit out the night before. Then again, had he known they'd be tardy he might've made proper plans to avoid the mishap. If only she wore uniforms to school, the decision would've been seamless. He scanned her closet for something that wouldn't be judged or reveal his folly. His breathing increased while his patience decreased. As great as options are, they can overwhelm even the strongest man when pressed for time. "I gotta give away some of this stuff. This is borderline hoarding." Unable to afford the lapsed time, he minimized the importance of her looking yearbook fresh, snatched up the threads, and then returned to the lavatory to wash her face. Had he not thrown the clothes on the bed he would've dropped them as his jaw fell. "Kayla!!" Her body flinched from the unexpected sound of his voice. Why was it so aggressive? That typically meant she had done or was doing something unapproved. Nevertheless, she locked eyes with him and waited for the revelation. "What are you doing???" She lifted her lathered hands as if to say, "Isn't it clear what I'm doing?" The water continued to splash and swirl around the achromatic basin as she waited for his reply. Her toothbrush, in arm's reach, was untouched and full of paste. He exhaled as his eyes rolled to the ceiling. Had he actually wanted her to wash her hands, she would've probably attempted to comb her hair or paint her toenails. He guided her hands under the water, rinsed them off, and proceeded to brush her teeth. "Let me see that big, beautiful smile!" Her cheerful expression was a thermostat of sorts, able to change the "temperature" from a moody room to a glee fest. He grinned and asked what she thought. She gave the thumb of approval. After her face was washed, clothes adorned, and shoes securely tied on her feet, he carried her to the car, activated the lift in the garage, and made haste like Lot leaving Sodom. As soon as he merged onto the highway a familiar sound reminded him that he decided to get gas the next morning, when he'd have plenty of time, instead of the night before when he didn't feel like it. After all, what would be the rush? "DAMN!" he struck the steering wheel with his dominant hand.

"Damn" her innocent angel-like voice echoed his sentiments from the back seat as she struck her tablet with both hands.

"No, No, Noooooooo." Remembering his precious cargo was in tow, "I said man. Daddy said, man."

"Damn," she repeated his original word. He refocused his breathing and mental state, then exited for gas, instead of risking the alternative: gassed out on the side of the road. He put just enough in to make it to the school and back to the nearest station. Back in the ride, he scurried along; his mind raced as well, "You had ONE job! You'll never hear the end of this. She'll drag it out like a last smoke" He flashed back to the conversation they had before left.

"Ok, I'ma need you to…" Myesha was interrupted by him snatching the paper out of her hand.

"You think you the only one that knows how to raise a child?! I ain't new to dis. I don't need a checklist or 'how-to guide.' Relax. We'll be fine. Enjoy your little girl's trip." His road down memory lane came to a halt when his phone rang. Of course, it was her. "Not now playa, not now." He let it ring so she wouldn't assume he sent her to voicemail.

"Mama" Makayla's arms stretched towards the center display with her mother's face on it. "I wanna talk to Mama." He turned but didn't say a word. "I wanna talk to Mama."

"We'll call her back when you get out of school." He attempted to pacify her, "I promise." She pouted as he swerved into the parking lot. "What THE…" he caught himself just in time. His daughter, now raised in the car seat, struggled to see what he was peering. What had his attention and caused his change of tone? "Is this the twilight zone? Am I being pranked?" He mumbled. "Did they evacuate?" His voice raised, "Where's everybody at?"

"Where dey at?" she restated.

He pulled over, gathered his senses, and checked his phone. It was Saturday. When the laughing subsided, he sighed. "Alright, that's it. No more brownies or gummies for me."

"I want a brownie" his baby requested.

That's the Good Stuff Favorites

Clayton Poland (Intro)

I have a confession. My brain functions like an old-school Rolodex; storing stories, quotes, illustrations, metaphors, bible verses, analogies, and random tidbits of information. Then during my day, something causes the ole Rolodex memory bank to spin, retrieving the perfect nugget to share in that moment.

This is a blessing and a curse. A blessing because it's great to be able to retrieve relevant content that could benefit someone or enhance a discussion. Or to say something funny to make people laugh or add a little levity to a tense situation. However, it can also be a curse because no one wants to come across as "Mr. Know It All" who has a story for everything. Through the years, I've learned to temper the use of my brain's Rolodex to balance out the blessing and curse.

From a very early age, I was fascinated with stories. I grew up in the South, a region known for birthing many great storytellers. And I wanted to be one of them! As Mark Twain famously said, "I like a good story well told. That's the reason I'm sometimes forced to tell them myself."

That's The Good Stuff is a collection of mostly true stories from everyday life, for everyday life. These stories are a myriad of personal stories collected from traveling nearly a million miles on the road with my family, plus a fresh take on familiar stories, tall tales, and parables, from today as well as days gone by.

As an homage to one of my storytelling heroes, Paul Harvey, each story ends with "That's the good stuff." I hope as you share these stories with your friends, family, and colleagues, they add a little shot of positivity and happiness to everyone's day. Use them in your meetings, messages, keynotes, or as motivation for your team.

I am pleased to grant my fellow author, Roland Moore, permission to include these stories in his upcoming book titled "*Flash Fiction Potluck*" While Roland has my full consent to use these stories, the ownership of the stories remains with me. I am excited to see how these tales will contribute to the rich tapestry of his work.

Enjoy my friends!
Clayton

The Good Stuff Disclaimer

The "I heard a different version" disclaimer: Each That's The Good Stuff story is a short story that's mostly true. Many of the stories are 100% true and told exactly as they happened, while others are entirely fictitious. So yes, I realize different versions of these fictitious stories could be floating around. If you've heard a different version, feel free to let me know. Just keep in mind, even if some of the particulars vary, the principle behind the story, well my friends, that's the good stuff!

Citation Disclaimer

Whenever applicable, I cite the source where I originally heard or read some version of the story. Over the years, I've collected these stories from books, online sources, and movies, as well as the many amazing storytellers I've met as I've traveled this great land. Nearly all of these non-personal stories fall under the category of common knowledge or common usage. That said, each story presented in this volume is a unique creation written the way I often present them to audiences.

The One About Houdini

Houdini parades into town with all the pomp and pageantry one would expect from the world's greatest magician.

His goal - to break out of their newly constructed, inescapable prison.

Once alone in the prison cell, Houdini pulls a solid steel bar from his overcoat and goes to work.

After 30 minutes, his pace quickens.

"There must be a weak point somewhere!"

After an hour, sweat is dripping from Houdini's brow. After two hours, Houdini collapses against the door of the prison cell...and the door opens. You see the warden had never actually turned the key to lock Houdini's cell. But in Houdini's mind, the door was as good as locked.

People debate the truth of this story. Fact or fiction, many times...we're just like Houdini. Locked in a mental prison of worst-case scenarios.

The key that unlocks our mental prison - is a new perspective.

A new perspective turns our biggest problem into our biggest solution.

Think about your family.

Your business?

Your relationships?

Your organization?

A new perspective is the key that will set you free!

And that my friends, that's the good stuff!

Citation: I originally heard this story from Zig Ziglar but have also read many versions online. Some say the story is fabricated. Others believe it to be true. Either way, the principle resonates well with audiences.

The One About the Cobra Effect

Colonial India was overrun with deadly cobras. The British government offered a bounty for dead cobras.
Initially, it worked, and the cobra population began to decrease. But entrepreneurial-minded Indians figured out they could breed cobras and turn them in for the bounty.
Realizing the cobra population was growing, the British government stopped the bounty.
With the bounty payments gone, the Indians released their cobras.
And you guessed it, the cobra problem got worse!
This phenomenon became known as The Cobra Effect.

When your attempted solution creates an unexpected problem.

There are other examples of The Cobra Effect with rats in Vietnam and feral hogs in Georgia.

The Cobra effect: When your attempted solution creates an unexpected problem.

What if we flipped the Cobra Effect on its head? Rather than looking for unexpected problems; what if we pondered the unintended benefits of a situation?

How could your current problem - benefit your life, family, business, or relationships?

What can you learn during a stressful time, that could make you better, stronger, faster for the next time?

When you figure that out my friends, that's the good stuff!

Citation: The Cobra Effect is a well-known and well-documented concept within economics with numerous case studies from a variety of sources.

The One About Good Will Hunting

Will, a troubled young man, sat across from Sean, his court-appointed therapist.

"I'm not going to get too close to my girlfriend because I'll find out she's not perfect."

Sean tells Will something embarrassing that his wife used to do in her sleep.

Then adds, "Will, my wife's been dead 2 years and that's the stuff I remember. Other people see these things as imperfections, but oh no Will...that's the good stuff!"

The impromptu scene was so powerful that the producers of 1997's Good Will Hunting left it in the film.

I agree with Sean - our imperfections are the good stuff!

Life is a mosaic - a big picture made up of individual snapshots in time.

From a distance, all our lives look perfect but when we zoom in, we see the imperfections.

Every family has moments that they'd rather not talk about or wish never happened.

Life's not always perfect. It's not always unicorns and rainbows.

A meaningful life is built upon viewing our tough moments, not as imperfections, but as the good stuff.

Our imperfections make us real, authentic, and relatable.

And that my friends, that's the good stuff! Citation: This powerful scene was filed away in my brain's Rolodex when I first watched Good Will Hunting. When I learned Robin Williams adlibbed this interaction, it made the principle all the more powerful for me.

The One About the Woah Person

Have you ever had a conversation with someone and no matter how hard you try, they don't understand you?

One key to effective communication is understanding the other person's perspective. Here's a simple personal example: I'm what's known as a Woah! Person. "Woah! You won't believe the idea I just had!"

My wife is also a Woah Person. But she's more Woah? "Woah? Are you saying you want to sell one of our kids and move us to the rainforest?"

I'm always excited about my next big idea. I couldn't care less about the details.

My wife is all about the details and can't love an idea until she has the details.

This "Woah" concept works for every relationship you have...personal or professional.

Think about the people in your life...which Woah person are they?

Too often we struggle to connect because we think everyone should see the world as we see it. So the next time you're struggling to connect with someone, ask yourself, "Which Woah person are they?"

It's a simple, effective way to see life from their perspective.

And that my friends, that's the good stuff!

Citation: This full idea is fleshed out in my TEDx Talk – Building a Culture of Family. You can find it on YouTube.

The one about Antoine Yates

Antoine had some strange habits. Some had even landed him in the emergency room. After one such visit, the doctors were so concerned about the holes in his arm...and frankly, the holes in his story, that they asked the police to check out his apartment.

The strange noises from the apartment forced the police officers to take a closer look.

And that was when they saw a 500-pound Bengal Tiger.

It was this pet tiger that sent Antoine to the emergency room after biting his arm.

Antoine thought it was completely normal to live with a fully grown, 500-pound Bengal tiger.

So here's the question - what's your tiger?

What's the thing you've gotten comfortable with that you actually never should've started in the first place?

Romans 12:9 reminds us to "Hate what is wrong. Hold tightly to what is good."

Bad habits start small but, over time, they grow into a 500-pound Bengal tiger.

Let's get rid of the sinful habits we've held onto before they destroy us.

Getting rid of our tigers and holding tightly to what is good, that my friends, that's the good stuff!

Citation: This story is well documented online. Antoine has lived a unique life that's for sure!

The One About the Wah-Wah Machine

A favorite childhood memory was watching the Charlie Brown holiday specials.

The Great Pumpkin, A Charlie Brown Christmas...I even like the Thanksgiving and Easter specials.

When Charles Shultz created Charlie Brown, he wanted the voice of the adults to sound like what kids heard, when adults spoke.

A trombone player supplied that old familiar "Wah-Wah" sound.

When the Peanuts movie came out, they created a website called the Wah-Wah Machine that spit out any phrase in the Charlie Brown teacher's voice.

When we don't connect as a family, we become the Wah-Wah Machine.

Tempers flare. Hearts are worn on our shirtsleeves and communication breaks down. The Harvard Study of Adult Development has followed the same group of individuals since the 1930s and they've discovered the key to long-term health and happiness is the quality of our relationships.

Relationships matter.

And the relationships we have with those we spend the most time with should be given the utmost care and attention.

Avoid becoming the Wah-Wah Machine.

Spend meaningful time nurturing the relationships with your family!

Because that my friends, that's the good stuff!

Citation: This idea is fleshed out in my TEDx Talk – Building a Culture of Family. You can find it on YouTube.

The One About the Logo on the Moon

In the 90's, Pizza Hut was brainstorming ideas
to share their new logo.
The chief executive boldly shared his out-of-this-
world idea.
"We're going to build a laser to project our logo
onto the moon!"
No one said what everyone was thinking
It took the astronomers and physicists to bring
Pizza Hut down to earth.
"Your laser would need to be the size of Texas
to make your logo visible from Earth."
Pizza Hut abandoned the laser idea but
eventually attached their logo to a NASA rocket.
Proverbs 16:3 encourages you to "Commit to the
Lord whatever you do, and he will establish your
plans."

Our dreams may seem out of this world, but when we follow the Lord's guidance, He establishes our plans. His plans align our dreams with His purpose for our lives.

When people tell you your dream is ridiculous, remind them of Pizza Hut. I bet your dream is nowhere near as crazy as putting a logo on the moon.

Commit your plans to the Lord, because that my friends, that's the good stuff!

Citation: I forget who first brought this story to my attention, but I do remember thinking there's no way it was real. I mean, other than Batman, who thinks a logo on the moon is a plausible idea? However, to my surprise, this story is well documented.

The One About the Golden Buddha

The Burmese Army set their sights on plundering the massive golden Buddha statue. To protect their beloved statue, the monks covered it with plaster so it would look ordinary. The army invaded, saw the ordinary-looking statue, and ignored it.

Centuries later, the government attempted to move what they assumed was a lightweight plaster statue.

The lifting straps snap, sending the statue crashing to the ground, cracking its plaster casing and exposing the gold.

Revealing what had long been forgotten - the statue was golden.

Ephesians 2:10 reminds us that we are God's masterpiece. Created in Christ to do good works.

Sadly, the pressures of life cause us to build a protective armor of stone over our lives.

The result is we believe we're an ordinary plaster statue and not a golden masterpiece.

Until something comes along that cracks our casing.

Maybe it's an injury, a divorce, a financial setback, a family emergency.

Something cracks our armor forcing us to remember the truth we've forgotten.

Living as God's golden masterpiece is key to a full life!

And that my friends, that's the good stuff!

Citation: I first came across this story while studying The Hero's Journey by Joseph Campbell. The Golden Buddha is on display in Bangkok, Thailand.

The One About the Dream

The most popular speaker in the world stepped
to the mic ready to call people to higher
standards.

However, today his message was missing his
usual punch.

That's when Mahalia Jackson yells to her friend,
"Tell 'em about the dream!"

The outburst startled the most popular speaker
in the world.

He took a breath, relaxed, and began to speak
with the passion and cadence of an old-school
Baptist preacher.

Dr. Clarence Jones realized, "These people
don't know it, but they're about to be taken to
church."

The most popular speaker IN the world delivered one of the timeliest messages FOR the world!

Dr. Martin Luther King Jr told the world, "I have a dream!"

Four words became the rallying cry of a nation.

Four words cut from the speech the night before, because many on his team felt it was tiring.

But those four words and their vision were in the heart of Dr. King.

They were never fully expressed until Mrs. Jackson screamed, "Tell 'em about the dream Martin!"

Out of the overflow of the heart, the mouth speaks.

And that dream my friends, that's the good stuff!

Citation: I discovered this little-known story of MLK's most iconic speech in a documentary featuring Dr. Clarence Jones.

The One About Even If Friends

The herald reminded everyone of the King's edict...worship the image or face the Furnace. The king rose from his throne, looked to his musicians, and gave the command to play! Instantly everyone bowed to worship the king's statue. Everyone that is, but three friends.

They knew the choice wasn't between the Image and the Furnace. It was between the Image and their Heavenly Father.

Furious with rage, Nebuchadnezzar demanded - "Last chance or face the furnace!"

In Daniel 3:16-18 the friends responded, "Oh King, we believe God will save us. But, EVEN IF he does not, we will not worship you or your statue."

Three EVEN IF friends were brave enough to stand for God when everyone else was bowing down.

Do you have any Even If friends?

Friends who'll walk with you through life's deepest, darkest valleys?

Here's a tougher question - are you an even-if-friend?

Do you have people in your life who could call on you in their time of need?

We need to become the type of friend we'd like to have.

Having and becoming an Even If friend, well...that's the good stuff!

Citation: This is another great passage of Scripture with many applicable truths for us today.

The One About My Swimming Pool

One hot summer, when my oldest son was 6, we built an above-ground swimming pool.

The anticipation on his young face was all the motivation needed to finish the project.

Being men, we scrapped several components we felt were unnecessary. Namely the instructions.

Watching my son swim in the pool for the first time filled me with joy!

Until it began to thunder...loudly.

There were no clouds in the sky, so it took me a second to realize it wasn't thunder.

The rumbling was the vibrations of the metal pool walls. In the blink of an eye, the pool collapsed!

10,000 gallons of water gushed out, with Ethan surfing atop the tidal wave.

He loved it and begged, "Can we do that again!"

I, on the other hand, felt like the biggest failure as a dad. My shortcuts could've hurt Ethan badly.

I needed to learn what Zig Ziglar famously said, "Failure is an event. Not a person!"

We all experience failure at some point in our lives.

Our failures make us human. Overcoming failure makes us stronger.

And that my friends, that's the good stuff!

Citation: Do you have a big failure in your past? If so, don't let it control your future.

The One About the Tire Shop

The mom walked in lugging a baby with two preschoolers in tow. She sat with the other patrons in the tire shop and began to scroll through her phone.

The preschoolers sat quietly for a moment, before they began to tear the place to shreds, climbing over everyone and everything.

All the while, the mom played on her phone, randomly shouting, "I can't wait for your daddy to get here!"

This scene increased in ridiculousness until the dad arrived and took the kids with him.

I shared the story with my kids while driving them to a department store.

Once inside I said, "You can have whatever you want! Thank you for not treating your parents the way the kids treated their parents."

I spent $25 on a doll, an action figure, and some food.

That 25 dollars literally changed how we parent.

We began to reward the behaviors we wanted to see replicated.

I encourage you to reward the behavior you want to see replicated!

Sometimes the biggest lessons are learned from others' mistakes.

Reward good behavior my friends because that's the good stuff!

Citation: The series of events live rent-free in the minds of my family.

The One About the Second Most Popular Song of All Time

Ole Jimmie stood on the platform listening as his opponent ripped him to shreds.

Everyone knew Ole Jimmie wouldn't retaliate. He never retaliated. He moseyed to the microphone atop his trusty steed Sunshine.

"Well folks, sounds like you just heard my life story. Not much to add...other than to sing you a song or two. So, gather 'round friends."

He took them home with the tune, Summertime before nailing them to The Old Rugged Cross.

But when he sang his most popular song, the second most popular song of all time, everyone sang along. They couldn't help it. It was just so catchy.

Ole Jimmie's most popular song is one of the most commercially produced numbers in American music.

Usually coming in second to Amazing Grace, arguably the most popular song of all time.

So, what song did the crowds demand their singing cowboy governor sing?

It's the song that became the state song of his beloved Louisiana.

A song you've undoubtedly sung ad nauseam while rocking a sleepy baby.

You Are My Sunshine. Written, performed, and made famous by LA Governor, Jimmie Davis.

That song my friends, that's the good stuff!

Citation: This story can be found in Jimmy Davis' autobiography: You Are My Sunshine.

The One About California's First Millionaire

In May of 1848, businessman Samuel Brannan heard "There's gold in them there hills!"

After checking it out, he brought a small bottle filled with said gold home and ran through the streets, shouting, "Gold! Gold from the American River!!!

A month later, three-fourths of the male population had moved to the mines.

Samuel saw his opportunity, not in the mines, but in providing resources for the miners: the soon-to-be well-known San Francisco 49ers.

Each day Brannon sold upwards of $5,000 worth of shovels, pans, and picks. The equivalent of $120,000 by 2020 standards.

His plan made him wealthier than the miners. It wasn't flashy. It wasn't noteworthy. But it worked...well.

So well, it made Samuel Brannan California's first millionaire.

The truth is that the gold rush merchants saw far more gold than most miners.

Don't overlook your idea because it's not as flashy as someone else's idea.

King David didn't build the Temple, but he did provide the building resources.

Samuel Brannan never dug for gold, but he made a lot of gold.

Your idea my friends, that's the good stuff!

Citation: This story is well documented from several sources.

The One About Jonah's Last Verse

My favorite example of God's love for children comes in the last verse of Jonah.

We all know the story. Jonah runs from God. Swallowed by a fish. Vomited on the shore. Preaches and the entire city repents. Jonah gets angry. He perches on a hill overlooking the city. There's a vine, a worm, and a mad prophet.

I mean Jonah tells God, "I'm so angry I could die!"

Jonah was mad about the whole turn of events. Yet in Jonah 4:11, God responds, "I'm concerned about this city, Jonah, because there's 120,000 people who don't know their right hand from their left."

How old were you when you knew your right hand from your left hand? 3? 4? 5 years old?

God wanted Jonah to understand he was
concerned for Nineveh because it was filled with
little kids. 120,000 kids who would grow up
without ever knowing of his goodness.

Jonah was sent by God to break this godless
cycle.

We'd do well to remember that God is still
concerned about kids today.

God showing love to 120,000 little kiddos, of
course, my friends, that's the good stuff!

The One About the Unsolved Mystery

The lady was nowhere to be found.

Her car was abandoned. Was it an accident? Or foul play?

Thousands searched from the ground while airplanes searched from the sky. Even the great Sir Arthur Conan Doyle, famed creator of Sherlock Holmes, couldn't solve the mystery.

The world held its breath as the search stretched out for 10 long, agonizing days. She was finally located safe and sound in a hotel spa under the alias Ms. Neele.

When asked for an explanation, the lady gave no answer.

The official diagnosis was "an unquestionable, genuine loss of memory."

The last 10 days were a mystery. The lady's response was a mystery.

The lady, already a famous novelist, would go on to write scores of mysteries.

Yet she never spoke of her mysterious 10 days, not even in her autobiography. 13 years later she released the gold standard for the mystery genre.

My favorite mystery novel - And Then There Were None.

By the greatest mystery writer of all time, who took her greatest mystery to the grave.

Agatha Christie.

Even in her death, she kept us guessing.

And that my friends, that's the good stuff!

Citation: This story is adapted from a short Netflix film about these events.

The One About Burning the Boats

Hernando Cortes recruited an extraordinarily committed crew.

Their mission - to capture the Aztec gold. Throughout the voyage, Cortes painted a vision of their future. "Your lives will never be the same! This fortune will change everything!" People had failed for 600 years to plunder the Aztecs, but Cortes was committed. He sold all his possessions leaving him only one objective - take the treasure. No plan B. Succeed or die! When they landed on the shores, the men awaited a motivational speech from their leader. Cortes offered just three words that motivated the men more than they could've imagined. Burn the ships!

The men realized if they were going home, they were going home in Aztec ships. As you probably guessed, the men fought well!

They took the treasure for the first time in 600 years.

The principle behind this story still holds true today - What are the boats we need to burn!?

What excuses are holding us back or keeping us from success?

Success comes when we fully commit and burn the boats!

When we do that my friends, that's the good stuff!

Citation: The truth of this story is debated. I've heard it presented by various keynote speakers over the years. Whether it's true or not, the principle of this story is very true.

The One About Father Damien of Molokai

Molokai is the 5th largest Hawaiian island.

An Eden-like paradise where Father Damien, a Catholic priest from Belgium, chose to spend his life.

Not on vacation but to serve the hundreds of lepers quarantined there from each of the Hawaiian Islands. Damien embraced them. Loved them. He ultimately gave his life for them.

While making tea one morning, boiling water splashed on Damien's foot and he realized he felt no pain. Dropping some on his other foot, he realized he had contracted leprosy.

That morning, rather than addressing "My fellow believers", Damien acknowledged, "My fellow lepers."

Everyone realized he was now one of them.

Upon his death in 1889, the Belgium government demanded the return of the body of their great hero.

But the people of Molokai pleaded, "Please consider sending some part of his body, some memory of his physical presence, for us to bury here?"

The authorities agreed to send his right arm to be buried in Molokai.

It was that arm that touched them and showed them the love of Christ.

Father Damien's legacy my friends, that's the good stuff!

Citation: The life of Father Damien is a saint within the Catholic Church whose notable life is well documented.

The One About Comparanoia

One Christmas I received a snowman-shaped yard tin from an unknown giver.

We don't collect snowmen but knew a mom in our church who did. I joyfully shared with this mom, "We don't collect snowmen, so here's one you can add to your collection."

She glared at me with sad puppy dog eyes and said, "I'll buy you another present if you want me to."

Yeah, that's right! I was trying to re-gift the snowman to the very lady who'd given it to me! People like and dislike this story for the same reason...it makes me look foolish.

We're so hesitant to admit our mistakes. We've become paranoid, especially in the age of social media. 24 hours a day, 7 billion people are waiting to tell us how we should look, talk and think. We've allowed too many voices to take up too much space in our lives.

When we compare ourselves to others until we become paranoid it creates Comparanoia.

Life is too short AND too long to live as a prisoner of Comparanoia.

Remember it's ok to laugh, especially to laugh at ourselves.

And that my friends, that's the good stuff!

Citation: I first heard this term used by my friend Tucker Stine.

The One About Mary Shelley

Mary's young life was marked by tragedy.
Her mother died when she was an infant and her
half-sister committed suicide. She often found
comfort in reading books while visiting her
mother's grave.

On vacation when she was 16, Mary and a few
friends entertained themselves by reading ghost
stories. They issued a challenge that each was to
write a ghost story to present the following
morning.

Her tragic life, coupled with haunting dreams
from the evening's ghastly stories, provided all
the inspiration young Mary needed.

The next day, the group agreed Mary's story
was, "Good for a girl." Not a knock about her
gender, but rather a compliment that a teenager
could pen such a fantastically original story.

Tragedy followed her as closely as her shadow. Her husband drowned and two of her children died. The desire to see her lost loved ones drove Mary to complete her novel.

A story about a fictional mad scientist who could do in print what Mary wished could be done in real life.

Bring her lost loved ones back to life.

That was the inspiration for Mary Shelley's - Frankenstein

Turning personal tragedy into triumph my friends, that's the good stuff!

Citation: My oldest son first mentioned this story leading me to research this story. This story is adapted from articles on History.com.

The One About the No. 2 Pencil

Here's a bold statement - no one person can make a No2 pencil.

It's true!

Where would you harvest the wood? How would you form the eraser? Can you mine the ore to make the metal ring to hold the eraser?

Once you molded the lead or graphite, how would you insert it into the wood? What glue formula would you use to hold everything together? What ingredients go into your paint? Think of the tools and machinery needed to collect and combine these simple elements into what we know as the basic No2 pencil.

We take for granted the legions of people, people who've likely never met, that must work together to produce something as special as a No2 pencil.

If cooperation is needed to produce a simple pencil, how much more cooperation is needed to produce healthy relationships, work environments, families, organizations, and churches?

1 Corinthians 12:12 tells us a body has many parts but forms one body. Let's learn to value and appreciate all the gifts within the body of Christ.

When we do that my friends, that's the good stuff!

Citation: This story is adapted from an essay by Leonard Read and an illustration given by economist Milton Friedman.

Clayton's Story

Clayton is a civil engineer turned author, speaker, and storyteller who encourages folks to focus on the good stuff in life. For him, the most important good stuff is family. In fact, much of the inspiration and stories he delivers to companies, organizations, and educators are rooted in spending almost a million miles on the road with his wife and kids over the years navigating life as a family.

He married his high school sweetheart, Leigh, and they have four amazing kids: Ethan, Maddie, Charlie, and Maria, their daughter from Guatemala. They call West Monroe, LA home and when he's not speaking and inspiring people across this great country, he can be found with family and friends enjoying his favorite foods and the wonderful culture of family they've built together.

Invite Clayton to your next event!

Clayton is a talented author, evangelist, and storyteller who encourages audiences to focus on the good stuff. His events combine fun, family-friendly humor, encouragement, and life-changing truth. His down-home delivery coupled with his energetic style and unbelievable stories reach people of all ages from all walks of life.

For more information, visit ClaytonPoland.com.

A Long Walk Home

Togenius Rabb

Work was hard, but it was finally over. Barnabas Asher began to prepare for his journey home. Satisfied by the work he'd dedicated himself to, he placed a bag over his shoulder; baggage he'd carried for a long time. The bag, once seen as a burden, had become barely noticeable. That was due, in part, to the soft-spoken and loving words of his mother. "Barney, when you focus on the baggage, you'll only magnify it. Our mindset determines the outcome of every situation."

That was one of the many seeds of wisdom his mother had imparted to him, and he held it dear to his heart.

Barnabas, a stickler of routine, stopped by a package store to purchase a few bottles of water for the walk home. It was common practice for him to keep water readily available. He was often told as a child that the water would protect him from the scorching heat. He set a bottle aside, placed the rest in his bag, then exited the store. Minutes into the trek, he bumped into a peculiar man he presumed was a vagrant. "Pardon me, kind sir!" the man muttered. "I was wondering, if at all possible, could you spare a bottle of water?"

"Sure," Barnabas replied. He handed him a bottle of water from his bag.

"Thank you, sir! The kind gesture is greatly appreciated." The peculiar man spoke with excitement. Barnabas simply nodded, smiled, and resumed his travel. "Thanks again!" Barnabas heard from a distance. When he turned to wave at the man, he observed him smirking as he poured out the entire bottle of water on the ground. Barnabas, confused and offended, once again was reminded of his mother's wisdom. "Barney Baby, you can't give your pearls to swine, they won't appreciate it." He regretfully turned and continued his journey. Eager to return home, he quickened the pace despite his fatigue. His haste was brought to a halt at the sound of women tittering through the glass of a sketchy-looking storefront. One of the women pounded on the glass and pointed to a sign that read '**Enter and we'll satisfy your every desire**.' Tempted, Barnabas began to consider the words of his father, "Son, a man who engages with strange women, freely gives away his honor. Do not give yourself to them, whose sole purpose is to distract and to stop you from elevating." Seemingly reluctant, he turned away, but not before sneaking another glance at the mesmerizing assortment of beautiful women seductively smiling at him through the glass. With one eye closed and the other attempting to capture a last glimpse, he redirected his focus and scampered along.

As he approached the last leg of his journey, almost home, his excitement grew. When he started to consume another bottle of water, a group of undesirables emerged from an alleyway. The thought of diverting from his route occurred as his level of consternation grew. Barnabas thought to himself, "Though I walk through the valley of the shadow of death, I will fear no evil: for You are with me; Your rod and Your staff shall comfort me." Confident in this, he pressed forward. As he neared the group, there was a sudden change in the weather. The sky began to darken, and a storm began to manifest. Strong winds and heavy rain began to arise. Barnabas sought shelter under an awning of a nearby storefront as he searched for an umbrella in his bag. When he tried to retrieve the umbrella, the remaining water bottles fell from his bag. He kneeled to pick up the bottles of water. When he arose, he became unsettled at the fact he was surrounded by the sketchy individuals he'd initially been apprehensive about.

"We were wondering if you had any water to spare. We're extremely thirsty." A member of the group spoke for the rest. "What would you exchange for the remainder of your water? Money? Perhaps women?" Two females walked from the back of the group to the forefront. "Food or even shelter from the storm?" Another chimed in.

As the heaviness of the rain increased and thunder roared throughout the sky, Barnabas, apprehensive and intrigued by the proposition, declined the offers, and cited the wisdom of his father "Beware of those who are set in your path to present fear, distract, and rob you of your valuables. Remember life is short and swift like a vapor in the midst, and those who are not as diligent would rather take from you to impede your progress and relegate you to their level." Barnabas opened his umbrella and confidently passed through the crowd.

As Barnabas' destination neared, the vicious storm started to subside, clouds began to disperse, and the rain suddenly stopped. He shook off his umbrella, placed it in his bag, and took out the final 2 bottles of water. He consumed one and placed the other on the steps of a local church. A feeling of relief set in as Barnabas realized that the rest was merely minutes away. Wet, ragged, and ruined, he tossed the baggage that he'd carried for far too long and tossed it in a nearby dumpster before entering the gates of his residence. With a sense of victory and accomplishment, Barnabas Asher uttered these final words, "I made it home! I finished my day with joy. Today I have overcome the world!"

Shoeshine

(Excerpt from "Flash Fiction a La Mode")

Duke and Todd were having a conversation as if William was invisible. It'd been a typical conversation about life after the war and what the future of America was. And by America, they meant the whites. They didn't respect the Negro very much. Blacks were a fourth-class citizen in their eyes. On their totem pole, it was: Successful whites, middle-class whites, lower-class whites, then Negros. They'd shared their perspective on several topics, from coloreds serving in the military, segregation, jobs, Jackie Robinson signing with the Brooklyn Dodgers, and UFO sightings.

"Make sure to put a good shine on em," Duke directed William, "I have an important meeting later on this evening."

"Yes sir," William replied without looking up. As a part-time boot shiner, he was privy to all types of conversations, thoughts, and philosophies. Some were beneficial and others meaninglessly ignorant. It was rare that any of them triggered negative emotions, and this one was no different. The nonsense went in one ear and out the other.

"A colored man shouldn't be in a position to lead white troops or make major decisions," Todd responded to Duke, "That's just too much pressure for their intellect." He looked down at William and added, "No disrespect but history and science just prove that we're better leaders."

Still diligently shining shoes, William waived his righthand up at Todd, "None taken, sir, I understand." William was a true professional, courteous, and rarely lost his bearing. He'd served in the war that the other two only pontificated about. From 1942 until the war ended, he valiantly contributed to his country. He, along with many other African Americans, were disappointed but not dumbfounded, to return home and still be treated as and considered less. Even the employment opportunities were less than desirable and available, for some of the same jobs they'd mastered and performed overseas.

"If they'd just learn a skill, they'd be hired like the next man," Duke assured all who could hear. "You can't be lazy in America and think you can get ahead." Ironically, there was a hint of truth in his statement. His parents had provided the best schools, financial support, and even reliable contacts, but due to his slothfulness, he'd gone backward and squandered the head start he was afforded in life. William, on the other hand, was an industrious gentleman who'd acquired some impressive skills before and during his enlisted time.

"There we go," William finished an excellent polish and stood up, "Thank you both for your business and I hope I can be of some service to you both, in the future."

Duke glanced at his shoes, then back at William and nodded his head up in down, "Not bad, not bad at all, son." His facial expression revealed just how impressed he was with the great job. He paid the exact price and then explained, "I don't have any money for a tip, but I can give ya some advice that'll help your life."

"I'd appreciate that," William facetiously replied.

"Work hard, be grateful, save up and one day you might able to afford some nice things."

By the looks of it, and not just when he buffed boots, you wouldn't have guessed the type of financial position that William was in. His parents owned two successful businesses in Greenwood before they were destroyed during the hideous Wall Street massacre of 1921. He'd chosen to fly under the radar and keep a low profile due to that historically tragic event. He owned land and a prominent mechanic shop in the town. The locals assumed it was owned by a Caucasian and that he was simply one of the workers, but he was, indeed, the head honcho.

He'd worked on trucks, hummers, planes, tanks, choppers, and more while in the military. He was a natural-born handyman who honed his skills while abroad. His time in the war also helped shape his demeanor, speech, and mindset, while he learned to keep his enemies close, as they revealed their true hearts and strategies.

"Thank you for sharing those words of wisdom, sir," he replied to Duke. "I'll be sure to keep 'em close to my heart now," he sarcastically ended the conversation, then turned and gently greeted the next customer.

Yeah RIGHT

(Excerpt from "How to Uplyft your earnings and receive Uber Tips")

One time, I was heading to one of my favorite pickup spots. It was a tavern on the edge of the city limits. The patrons that become passengers there usually take care of you. They normally never travel far. They're responsible and wise in catching a ride no matter how close their homes are. One night I took a passenger three minutes up the street and he tipped me $80.

This night I picked up a couple. The man appeared to be slightly older than his wife. You could tell that she had some work done by the way things were sitting. Their house was seven miles towards town from where we left. After we exchanged pleasantries, they briefly talked amongst themselves about the night. He started talking to me when we were about a mile away from their address. GPS isn't always spot on, especially in newer or less traveled areas, so I slow down the closer I get to a final stop. There was a familiar fancy neighborhood on the left. So logically, I assumed that's where they lived. As we neared the neighborhood he said, "That's us up there on the right." They didn't seem that intoxicated but clearly something was off because on the right, not too far ahead, was a shopping center. You could tell by the way the lights reflected off the building. Then his wife chimed in, "Not the first entrance but the second."

My thoughts: Ooooooh KAY. They want me to turn into the shopping center. Perhaps they left their vehicle there.

It turns out they did leave their vehicle there, along with their other cars, clothing, furniture, appliances, and lawn. It indeed was their house, not a shopping center. They had their own gated community with two entrances and speed bumps. Not sure who the speed bumps were for but who am I to tell someone how to accessorize their driveway? Have you ever met someone with so much money or luxurious things that you instantly humbled yourself and reset your thought process? I left their gated estate, thinking to myself, "Is what I have even considered money to them?" Then I laughed all the way up the street.

Abortion Clinic Chronicle

(Excerpt from "Flash Fiction Feast")

It was as soundless, as expected. There was no television in the waiting area, or radio station playing over the intercom system; just a few informational posters and pictures on the wall. And of course, brochures near the receptionist window and tables in the sitting area. Chris had never been in an abortion clinic, and he sat there as quiet as the others while waiting for Lishay's name to be called. I guess there isn't much to talk about once you've made it that far in your life-changing decision. Plus, who really knows abortion lounge etiquette? Unless maybe, you worked the front desk or frequented those establishments for other reasons. Lishay was a novice "visitor" as well.

She'd actually been there once in support of a close friend who made a similar choice, but never for herself. As a matter of fact, she never would have imagined in a thousand years that she would be there for herself. After all, she had been taking birth control pills since her first and only son was born. She figured that taking an oral contraceptive would prevent any further premarital "mishaps" from coming to light. Clearly, she miscalculated or put too much trust in an anovulatory drug. What she wasn't about to bank on, was Chris making an honest woman out of her because she was expecting. He never married or made mention of the thought, when it came to his other two children's mothers. He had two daughters from previous relationships with two other women. As much as Lishay loved

Chris, she was unwilling to become his third baby's mother or have two baby daddies'.

"Thank you for bringing me," Shay softly uttered.

"You're welcome," Chris maundered. He was happy she had broken the uncomfortable silence and at the same time frustrated that he didn't know what to say to keep the conversation going. He gently grabbed her hand in an effort to communicate nonverbally with her. He loved Shay and was content with how their relationship was progressing, but this was definitely a stunning turn of events. His impregnating her was the last thing on his mind. And why would it be at the forefront of his thoughts? She was on birth control and had made it ever so clear that she was NOT trying to have another child before she was married.

From her actions, she wasn't trying to quit having sex either. They say you don't know what you're missing until you've had it. Coitus embodies that statement to the third degree. Raw sex personifies it in the first degree. It felt exulting for Chris to be able to "shoot the club up" any time of day, with no fear of it coming back to haunt him. And it was reassuring for Shay to have all the pleasure of unprotected sex without worrying about the physical or emotional pain of birthing a love child. Her comfort tragically vanished the day she realized she was preggers.

"I'm pregnant," Shay revealed during a face-to-face talk.

"Pregnant??" Chris confusedly replied. "How can that be? Aren't you on birth control? Are you sure? Did you take a test?" Shay cut him off before he reached twenty-one questions, "Yes, I'm sure. I don't need to take a pregnancy test. I've been pregnant before and I know what it feels like." At that point, Chris was still baffled at the news and in denial.

"How can you be pregnant when you're on birth control?" he retorted.

"When I was sick and taking those antibiotics, they must have interfered with the birth control," she answered. "That's one of the warnings when taking the pills."

"Warnings? WARNINGS?" Chris internalized to himself, "It would have been nice if she had told me that. Why would she not say anything so we could have taken precautions?" he reasoned within. "So, are you going to take a test to be certain?"

"I missed my period weeks ago and I know what it feels like, but I will take one for you to confirm what I already know." Reality was setting in for Chris. He knew Shay wasn't the type to play games or tell false tales.

Nevertheless, he replied, "Yeah, take one to be sure."

"I'm not keeping it," Shay interposed. "I just wanted to let you know. I already thought about it enough and made my decision." Chris' eyes said, "OH!" though verbally he was hush.

"I'm not telling you for any money either; my brother James is going to lend it to me," Shay informed him. James was her half-brother whom she didn't find out about until she was out of high school. They had become purposefully close since then and she knew she could count on him for the money and more importantly to not tell a soul. She had two full brothers who were able to help financially at a moment's notice, but she didn't feel they could handle it mentally or emotionally. "I just want you to go with me," she added.

"Lishay Johnson?" inquired the lady who opened the doorway to a hall that led to the back rooms. Shay let go of Chris' hand and stood up. Neither made eye contact as she walked off. Shay had told Chris approximately how long it would take, and that if he wanted to leave, he could come back around that time, or she would call him when it was done. Shortly after the door was securely shut behind Shay, Chris took a deep breath and got up.

"Should I go stop her?" Chris wondered inwardly. Although Shay had laid out the plan for everything, he never once tried to overrule or talk her out of it. He never expressed to her that he wanted a son and how he felt strongly that she was carrying his. Was he messing up by not trying to convince or at least show her that it would be better if they had the child? Would it be overly dramatic if he busted in or beat on the door and yelled to prevent it? Would he be considered crazy at the minimum or worst-case scenario, go to jail for such an act? As he walked toward the door, Shay slowed down and looked back at the same door from the other side. It was as if both of them wanted the other to say or do something before it was ultimately too late. Chris reached for the door handle, then turned and went in the direction of the exit and left the building. Both doors were near one another in such a small-scale clinic. He sat in his car, drained and bemused, with key in pocket, for the duration; debating within himself if he had messed up by not stepping up. Shay lay stiffly on the bed that seemed more like a cold table for cadavers in a mortuary. Things would never be the same.

What's good for a headache?

(Excerpt from "How to Uplyft your earnings and receive Uber Tips")

They say you never forget your first. This is the first encounter that really stood out, so if I forget any other story, I'll never forget this one. I arrived to pick up a female at a popular bar downtown. We hadn't even driven one block when her phone rang. Here's how the conversation went:

Her: I just left the spot. I've been trying to reach you all night. I can't because I already ordered a ride and he's taking me home now.

Me: If you need me to take you somewhere else, I can. I don't mind.

Her: We're still downtown. Do you want to meet?

I initially thought it was her boo. But then I thought, "Why doesn't she just get out and he can come get her, or he can meet her at her place, or I can take her to his?"

Me: If it's easier, I can take you to him.

Her: He stays with his girl and kids.

My thoughts: Oh ok, she's the side piece.

I told her the best place to meet, he agreed, and we met there. We arrived there first. Soon after, he pulls up with tinted windows. She gets out, leaves her things in my vehicle, and says, "I won't be too long."

My thoughts: I hope this dude doesn't know me or think he knows me, or that I used to talk to the chick he's living with or someone he used to kick it with. I don't have time for no drama tonight.

About ten minutes later, she gets back in my ride, and we head to her original destination. Turns out, she was a bartender who had worked at a few bars over the last few months. And as a bartender, every night when she got off work, she hits another bar up to hang out and have drinks.

Me: Do you normally wake up with hangovers or has your body become accustomed to it and it's nothing?

Her: I still have hangovers some mornings.

Me: You should take some BC powder before you drink, that would probably knock it out.

Her: I can't, that powder doesn't sit right with my body. Aspirin either.

As I'm thinking of something else she can do or take to prevent hangovers, she says, "Can I ask you something?" in a bashful voice. Mind you, this whole time she's been talking bold and gritty as ever.

Me: of course

Her: Ugh, naw, never mind.

I'm not the nosey or overly concerned with much type but with such an extreme turnabout in her confidence, I was somewhat curious as to what she was thinking, concerning me.

Me: What is it? You're good. You don't have to be ashamed.

Her: OK…do you mind if I do a line?

Me: WAIT, you can't take BC powder, but you take cocaine powder???

I never knew a love like this

WOW! Will you look at that. I couldn't have planned it better if I tried. Lord knows I do. The love of my life, a mere bus link away from me. And to think, I thought this splendid day would fail to get better. At least not until I made it home. She was the early bird that beat me up and vanished before I could get situated this morning. Her flawless face, flowing hair, and sexiness roamed free in the depths of my mind all day. It's a wonder I got anything done. How I pine for her presence to surround me like a flounder out of water. Drink her bathwater? I want to BE her water. I want to be her air. I want to be everything she needs and beyond. She has no CLUE how deep my love runs for her. There's not enough chains in the world to keep me from her. If I died, I would come to her in a wet dream. Should I sneak up behind her now or surprise her later? How long will it be before she notices me? She rarely turns around on her walks. Can you blame her? Neither would I if I were the epicenter of fineness. I'd walk around like my butt never stinks. Like all eyes on me. I bet she stops by her favorite smoothie shop on the way home. If I were a betting man, I'd wager six weeks' pay. After all, who knows my baby more than me? Honestly, I'm just happy to not be taken for granted. My last love interest, the most ungrateful person on EARTH, wasn't worth an ounce of the effort I gave. I wish I never pursued her. Nevertheless, here I am. A new day, a new way. Happy life, happy wife, or however the saying goes.

"HEY!! Watch where you're going, STUPID!"

"Oh my GOSH!!" I can't stop my heart from beating. I almost lost my life not paying attention. Watching babe cross the street, instead of oncoming cars, nearly left me paved. Ok, OK, deep breaths. INHALE...EXHALE. Inhale...exhale. And look at her. None the wiser. Her Romeo inches away from comatose, and she didn't miss a beat. Earbuds on decibel levels not safe for an infant, but that's my baby and I wouldn't wish her any different. If she never changes a bit, I'll be happier than a suicide bomber in the afterlife with a hundred titts. Speaking of, hers are PERFECT. I only have eyes, thoughts, and desires for her supple, succulent, sweet, tender melons. If hers were the forbidden fruit, I would've fallen like Adam twice. Three times if it meant pollinating her flower and forever being near her nectar. Speaking of juices, I KNEW she was stopping by that shop for her drink. Tropical Chi with pineapples, kale, berries, and an energy boost. When you know you know. I can only guess how much she truly appreciates the details and memory space I allot to her. Let's see if I know her like I think I do. Yeah, let me stay outta sight and outta mind until we've taken further steps. Watch we look back on this and laugh, while she SWEARS she knew I was here all along, waiting for me to say, boo. Meanwhile, I'll just nod in agreement, fortunate to be with the one who many would say is out of my league. They could NEVER understand the soul tie we have. The bond that refuses to be broken. The two hearts beating as one. The sexy Ying and the quirky

Yang. How the first time peering into her beaming eyes, sparked a never-dying, unquenchable flame within the fiery fiber of my spirit. I'm blessed to be living for this but make no mistakes I'll DIE for us if ever put in that predicament. I'm not a killer, but please don't push me. But let me calm down. Sometimes I get in my own head and thoughts consume me. I need to keep the things my therapist shares with me at the forefront of my mind at all times. Positive thoughts lead to positive outcomes. Why focus on foreboding futures when I presently have so much to be thankful for? The cutest one, with the prettiest lips, smack dab in front of me. Let me stop before onlookers think I'm shaking my head in disgust and not delight. Plus, here we are, at the humble abode. Andddddd right on cue, is the annoying doorman doing the MOST, trying to flirt with MY woman. NEWSFLASH! No one likes to talk to you, BRO! She's only being nice since she was raised to be a wholesome woman of respect. Me on the other hand, if I EVER catch him off duty and alone, they'll be reading about him in the paper. BINGO, I got action! "Excuse me! Ma'am, you dropped your paper!"

"Oh my! Umm, thank you?"

"I'm sorry, Miss. I didn't mean to startle you. I just happened to be walking up and saw you dropped something. Didn't know if it might be important or not."

"It's not. It's just a receipt."

"Right, the smoothie in your hand. Of course. Well, I'll get out of your way. Nice to officially meet you, more or less. I stay in this building too. We're...we're...we're neighbors..."

Beyond the High Score

Dominic Murphy

"Check it, bro. I'm almost at the top score, right? All I need is 5,000 more points and I will be the highest scorer and you all will be… LOSER." Welston loved his games and loved boasting about how good he was. "You know what happens after I step over that high score buddy…" He stalled to listen for Ray to respond, "Oh, you're silent right now, but you know what happens. You can no longer call me by my government, my friend, because after I murder the 1mil point mark, you will have to call me Commander UBD." Welston yelled over the headset while gaming out of control with his best friend Ray.

"Do you really think they'll send you the brand-new Tactical Retrieve Virtual Command Center?" Ray asked as he twisted and turned his game controller to maintain the life of his avatar during the battle.

The newest popular game, Tactical Retrieve, had a strong grip on the gaming world. It was borderline cultic. The game was so popular that it transcended the gaming world in ways no one could have imagined. Welston was 5,000 points away from seeing how far the game bled into reality.

"OOHHH YOU CAN RUN, but you can't HIDE. Take these bullets for your medication." Weston was breezing through the game as if he designed it himself. It was like he knew what was coming next and the high score was within reach. He was so absorbed that he forgot he was not a real mercenary. Then without warning the screen went black. The only noise was his yelling and the pounding on the controller. "Oh no, bro! WHAT JUST HAPPENED!?"

Ray was still going so he had no idea what Welston was seeing or not seeing on his end. "What do you mean?" Ray asked but there was no response in the headset from Welston. "Wes? Are you there?" Ray paused the game and set his controller down on the bed. He pulled his phone out and dialed up Welston.

Welston stood before his television with a black screen and controller still in hand. His slumped shoulders and glazed twitching eyes showed his incredulity was maxed out. He felt like the 45-second time-lapse was an eternity since his screen blacked out. This unfortunate violation of his rise to the top would rile him like he's never been vexed before. The tantrum was starting to erupt with a viscous shaking of his head and yelling, "NO NO NO!" At the top of his lungs. The second he walked up to his television and grabbed the screen, it flicked on but the game that once dominated the monitor was no longer there. He was now staring at his avatar instead. The avatar guided him through a door and pointed at a desk. At the desk, sat the general with his back to the screen.

The general spoke as he stared out a huge window and puffed on a cigar. He reached out from his chair and tapped ashes into an ashtray. "So, Commander UBD. I see you have proven that you are ready." He continued staring out the window with his back to the screen, but he began to rotate around to face the screen while stating, "I must tell you, I am very impressed at how fast you rose to the top, but you know… That was just an audition." He puffed on the cigar and looked right into the screen. "Now it's time to see what you're made of…" He stood up from his chair, leaned onto his desk, and with a calm sonorous hum, rumbled, "For real!" There were only a select few who could boast about being part of a class of elite gamers and Welston had just become the newest member. The general told him he would now have to take out top priority targets for the government and if he opened his mouth about it, he would become a target. There was something different now about the game that made Welston very nervous and yet just as intrigued.

The gaming manufacturer advertised that eclipsing a certain score would set you apart from any old gamer. They promised the lucky ones, who achieved this feat, would receive the new high-tech virtual reality system called The Tactical Retrieve Command Station. This was beyond what the gamers were accustomed to. It came with a never-before-seen, state-of-the-art game console, virtual reality headset with goggles, a full-body suit, gloves, a stationary body platform, the size of a treadmill, and a "CONTRACT?! Why do I have to sign a contract?" Welston yelled as he read what came with the command station.

"In blood!" The general spoke as if he was responding to Welston's inquiry. This caused Welston to start looking around for cameras and microphones. He had never felt this before. Paranoia has never interrupted his joystick time. This was too much to continue but not enough to press the power. It was like the general was watching him from the screen. "Don't worry Commander UBD, there is nothing to find. You are not being watched, but you are being tested, and the final test will come after you answer the door."

Before he could even process what the General said, there was a knock at the door. This was outside of new and beyond creepy, but he couldn't escape game mode. He had to know what was next. He looked at the screen and asked, "What if I don't answer the door?" Curiosity fueled his query but any response from his television would enkindle trepidation.

"If you don't answer, you will never know what comes next. There will not be another knock, nor will there be another opportunity to know." The general puffed on his cigar, stared right into the screen, and continued with a firm hypnotic tone, "What... Comes... Next..." He looked at his watch and with a smile and expression that screamed coercion, "You have less than a minute to join my elite team, Commander."

Welston was stung with the need to know. He scampered from the basement toward the front door. The man on the other side of the door was dressed like a secret service agent but he had no equipment available. He stared at Welston through his dark shades for about 5 seconds before asking, "Are you Commander UBD?"

He stuttered and fidgeted around then responded, "Uhm, I'm Wel... uhm... Commander BD... uhm... DU...uhm... yes, I'm uhm.. him... yes, I am. Uhm, who's aski..."

Before he could finish his question, the man shoved three pieces of paper in his face and then shook his hand. The weird-looking ink pen in the man's hand accidentally poked Welston's hand and drew blood.

"Oh, sorry about that. He gave Welston an expensive handkerchief for the bloody finger and took the ink pen and contract back." He immediately turned and motioned to a white cargo van to bring the equipment.

From about half a block away Ray was racing on his bike yelling, "WELSTON...WEEELLLSSTOOONNN, DON'T DO IT."

The man ignored Ray and told Welston, "Read the contract and sign it before the next game starts. You have four hours until the start time. These men will set your command station up in the same room as your current game console." He pushed the door open and told Welston to lead the way.

Welston was conflicted between leading the way and waiting for Ray to reach the house, but the man told him, "I'll make sure to let him in once he arrives, but please lead them to the area for the setup."

Welston took the delivery men to the basement and hurried back up to meet Ray but when he got back upstairs, he saw Ray out on the sidewalk chatting with the man in shades before leaving on his bike. "What did he want? What did you tell him?"

"Nothing except that you're about to set up your command center and he knows what to do if he wants one." He took his Shades off, looked Welston right in the eyes, and said, "Now go set up your command station, Commander UBD, your next game starts in less than four hours." He tapped his wrist and whispered, "Tick Tock."

Welston was still confused but curious, so he asked, "Well, what's the next game?"

"Oh, you will find out soon enough. I have the signed contract and you have the equipment. Once they are done, you are going to put on your body suit and virtual headset. You will select the initial briefing and be SURE… to listen very carefully to the general's instructions."

Welston thought to himself, 'I never signed a,' then spoke as if to question, "Contract?"

"Yes, in blood to be exact." He pulled out the papers he originally gave Welston and took the weird pen then put two drops of Welston's blood on the signature line. "It's official. You're an elite killer… I mean soldier, now, and you belong to us."

Last Call

"I know you fucking lying," Leigh exclaimed. "You still talk to ole girl? The inquiry was rhetorical in nature. However, she was perplexed as to why.

"Why wouldn't I?" Lloyd often replied with hypophora. "I get all the benefits and none of the headaches. Plus, that 'Hawk Tua' is looney."

"I mean, who doesn't love some fiyah head," she acquiesced. "You don't ever worry about her fiancé finding out? Don't act like you forgot what happened to my cousin." An enraged boyfriend and the homies caught him slipping. They beat her relative beyond recognition. Physically, in due time, he recovered. Mentally, not so much. "You ready to

DIE for that pussy?" They locked eyes, without word for a few seconds, then simultaneous laughter reset the mood in the room to the accustomed norm.

"You and 'Bank' still good?" They used monikers for everyone they talked to. It made it easier to keep up with. Plus, who doesn't love a creative cute cognomen? Leigh had contacts like *DayCare* (several baby mamas) *ShortStop* (knew how to work it but didn't have enough) *Turtleneck* (uncircumcised) *Borrowed* (Married man. That was, of course, before her cousin's brutal incident) *Juvie* (the time she felt like a cougar) *Stephen A. Myth* (swore he was a sports expert but never won any parlays) *Norman B* (Psychotic mama's boy) *Hips, Purse Guy, Lunch Man, Old Bay,* and even *BATS* (Bitch Across The Street) stored in her phone.

"He's blocked right now." Her block game was Hall of Fame left tackle status. Before she could share why, Lloyd's phone rang. It was *Boomerang* (she always came back)

He walked to the balcony to answer. "Well, well, well. Look who decided to hit me back."

"I told you we were having date night before I left," Nicole replied.

"Indeed, you did but riddle me this, who's coming over when they're done playing party patty?" He wasted no time.

"I can't keep doing this with you. I have a good man who actually wants to be with me." She often tried to convince herself more than anyone else. She loved Lloyd like no other, but her friends and family kept imploring her to leave him alone. If they even suspected, although her best friend aka *Cover Girl* knew, she was still talking to him they'd blow their top like an overboiled pot.

"Yes you can," he insisted. "He don't do you like I do." Their intimacy was unmatched. No one made her feel like he could, in the bedroom, pool, back seat of the Wagoneer, or up against the balcony bars. "Don't be getting too drunk where you can't drive." She enjoyed drinking and having a good time.

"I only had one drink, and I didn't even finish that." Clearly being sober enough to drive at the end of the night was in her plans.

"That's what I like to hear. I have your favorites waiting for you. Just get your pretty little face here safe and we'll work things out until the AM."

"I think he's getting suspicious. Something's been on his mind all night. I can see it on his face. I'm not trying to ruin a good thing for you. It's not like you're ready to step in and step up if he finds out." She often offered ample opportunities for him to say he wanted to be in a committed relationship.

"We can talk about it when you get here." He didn't plan to talk much when she walked through the door. "Gone get back to him since you swear he's Detective Holmes now."

"Be cool, Lil Daddy. I got this. Just worry about what I said. I'm not gone wait around until I'm fifty. I'm way too good to you. You gone miss me when I'm gone."

"Where you going, baby Nicki?" He played dense to fluster her nerves.

"Boy, bye!" As usual, she failed to reach him when it came to serious matters. "If I stay in this bathroom any longer, he might come looking for me. At least someone cares about me. I'll text you when I'm on the way." She could sense his smile on the other end. "Don't get too happy. This the last time…"

Aqua Vitae

It can make you feel STRONG.

It can make you feel WEAK.

It can make you feel invincible.

It can kill your liver.

When you're young, it can make you last all night.

When you're old, it'll embarrass you. You'll need help getting up.

It can make you feel invigorated.

It can make you feel depressed.

It'll have you pontificating profusely.

It'll have you mumbling words like a sleepy toddler.

It'll make your worries go away.

It'll make you overthink and paranoid.

It could be used to celebrate.

It could lead to tragedy.

It'll have you reminiscing.

It'll have you forgetting.

It'll have you longing for it.

It'll have you swearing you'll never indulge again.

It'll have you hugging strangers.

It'll have you hugging a porcelain fixture.

It'll have you professing, "I love you!"

It'll have you swearing, "I HATE YOU!"

It'll have you up all night, partying until daylight.

It'll have you sleep all day, cringing at too much light.

It can free your inhibitions.

It can cost you your freedom.

It can lead to you seeing the truth.

It can cause your vision to be impaired.

It's why some families gather.

It's why other families feud.

It might enhance game night.

It might end games and start fights.

It's addictive to some.

It's repulsive to others.

It can help ease tension.

It can cause major pain.

It can be enjoyed while watching a movie.

It can have a movie watching you.

It can be popped and showered all over during championships.

It can be poured out while mourning a lost sister or brother.

A little can make your gut feel better.

A lot can make your stomach feel horrible.

It was recommended in the Word (1 Timothy 5:23)

It was warned about in the Word (Isaiah 5:11)

It can make you want to get up and go for a spin.

It can make the room spin without you moving.

People have studied it freely and made observations.

People have been ordered to take classes to avoid incarceration.

Some don't want to live without it.

Some must live without others because of it.

Some show it off in elaborate displays and cases.

Some hide it out of sight from nosey or
judgmental faces.

After a long day, some run to it.

Others take 12 steps to stay away from it.

One moment it can make you feel no shame.

In an instant, it can ruin your name,

It might go down smooth or be tough to
swallow.

You may throw it up violently, then toss and
wallow.

It can make you sociable.

It can make you unbearable.

It can be a multiplier of many things.

It can divide you from people or things you value.

It can make you react quickly.

It can drastically slow your reaction time.

It can encourage you to dance and have a ball.

It can make you lose your balance and fall.

An optimal amount can make you feel so alive.

Too much can "unalive" you.

The right amount can feel like a love potion.

The wrong amount can poison your organs.

What can it do for you?

What can it take from you?

Is it worth it all? Pardon the potable pun!

Lord, please!

"Lord, if you get me out of this one, I promise to do better." Bullets were flying overhead like planes leaving Hartsfield-Jackson Atlanta International. "Don't let me go out like this. Not today." Jackson inwardly pleaded with God. When the doors were kicked in, he instinctively took refuge beneath the crap table. He wasn't sure if the initial rounds were warning shots or specific individuals targeted. Were bystanders dropping their drinks from being hit or out of shock? Either way, glass shattered, screams erupted, and civilians scattered. Sonny's Sugar Shack had experienced run-of-the-mill fights, disputes, and debates from inebriated patrons and sore losers alike but never a full-on arsenal attack from outsiders. Sonny's security fired back. It sounded like a Fourth of July finale, but the fireworks were meant to do more than entertain. You couldn't tell if people were falling out from being hit, ducking for cover, or tripping over the furnishings. Jackson was practically in the fetal position, shivering like Jack talking to Rose while she floated on that door. Sonny's ship was sinking as well. Who would want to sabotage such a beloved establishment? Pound for pound it held its own against any national adult amusement business. Over the years it attracted "tourists" from around the globe, wanting to see if the stories were true. Were the dancers exotic and affable? Was the food five-star or better? Did the music match the elegant ambiance? Were the table games fair? Did the slot machines ring and flash more than not? Were your secrets kept private? Did the champagne sparkle and deliverers delight? People wanted to know. Jackson just wanted to live. His heart palpitated. He couldn't catch his breath. Sweat pelt down his body. His anal sphincter clenched like the fist of a stingy man. The chaos carried on for minutes, but it felt like an hour. He remained motionless for minutes in the aftermath. Once able to move, he looked side to side, then maneuvered like a sloth from under the table. The scene resembled the wreckage of a frat house the morning after an ungoverned party. Bodies, bottles, broken glass, chips, and blood were everywhere. Were others alive? He was unwilling to check. He'd fervently prayed for a way out and was ready to take it. However, before he crept toward the exit, a familiar pair of shoes caught his eye. He'd admired them during the dice game. He raised his head on high, "Lord, you know the heel spurs I have. I could use some comfortable shoes. I mean, it's not like he'll be walking anywhere on earth. Waste not, want not, right?" He tried them on. "Perfect fit." Not far from there was a Ziplock bag on the floor near the roulette table. "Thank You. You know I'm stressed. I can relax my nerves for the week. One man's loss is another man's treasure, right?" He tucked the cannabis in his back pocket. Feeling quite blessed, he decided to be a good Samaritan and see if maybe one of the dancing artists was injured or afraid, in their dressing room, and needed some help. No luck. You could tell they didn't delay. Everything but their life was replaceable. He noticed a Hermès Birkin bag that stood out from the rest. I peeked into it and found the matching wallet. In it was the driver's license of one of the sexist pole performers. "I should probably return this turn her. I mean at least see if she still lives at this address. Ain't no telling what these dirty cops a do when they find it. Plus, we need to do a better job of protecting our women. Then again, she might be a suspect. Either way, what would Your Son do? He'd leave the 99 to help the one, right?" He put the wallet in his front pocket. On his way out, he noticed a few vials. "I should check these in case it's some blood pressure or heart pills. We wouldn't want anyone to be in danger of dying." One was full of Soma. "Lord, you know I've been having back tightness. You're always on time." Another was 10mg of Percocet. "If this don't help my aching knee, nothing will." There was even a bottle of syrup in arm's reach. "I can finally get rid of this cough. He's a healer, He's incredible." He pointed and waved his hand to the ceiling. "Let me get outta here before the cops come or worse." On his way out he stopped by the coat room. "It might be colder out now, or later this month. You never know. I should be prepared like the virgins with that lamp oil, right?" He checked the inner left pocket while walking out. There were two wads of cash in it. He shook his head in disbelief. "Lord, You keep on blessing me. I'm putting some of this in the collection plate tomorrow." He hadn't been to church in years. In the other inside pocket were some condoms. "I get it. I hear You, Lord. If I so happen to fall, You want me to protect myself. Message received." He was on cloud nine. He floated to his ride.

He reached for the handle and heard, "STOP! If you even flinch, I'll blow Yo brains cross dis lot." The untimely stranger cocked the hammer. "Put your hands on your head."

He slowly raised his hands, eyes beginning to water, "Lord," he took a deep breath and closed his eyes, "I come to You as humble as always…"

I WILL be a Freeman

"Duh sun done burn him bad. Every man have a breakdown at some point. May he rest and be back skrong come sunlight morrow"

"I's be a freeman morrow!" Axum (slave name Charles) repeated what he'd been proclaiming for the last five minutes with confidence to Abasi (slave name Jim) and the others. "I get a vision from God during dee night. God no lie." He remained steadfast, somewhat scowling and shaking his head at Jim for making light of his shared revelation.

"It badder than I think. Someone get dis fool a drink…before he fall out and bring attention to us." They ALL needed to hydrate. Even mosquitoes found shelter in the shade. You could've set a cast iron skillet on their skin and fried eggs, so it was reasonable to think their brains were just as scrambled. Not that their self-appointed masters thought they had any. At least not the mental capacity of an All-American-blooded man. They deemed the melanated servants as less than human (soulless) and dumber than a dog (not smart enough to be loyal and thankful for a house out back and occasional scrapes from the table to feast on). Man's best friend drank water freely (sometimes from the same canisters as their owners) ate plenty and found shelter in the shade on the porch or the coolness of the house. An occasional nigger hunt would be the most strenuous "stress" their bodies would know. They were even buried amongst family and mourned for days. Not that slave masters weren't upset when their free help died. It was just for unsentimental reasons. No one enjoys spending money on fallen instruments of labor. Fortunately, their purchased or stolen tools reproduced, allowing for a lifetime of free labor.

"Take me with you," Jabari (slave name Virgil) entreated his worn but not broken ally Axum.

"Now dis tired fool make others have false hope" Abasi grew more and more frustrated as others began to believe that Axum had the answers they desired. "The only thing he take will be fifty lashes when Massuh catch him not far away." To his credit, he'd lived long enough to see it happen to several enthused escapees. The sounds of a man being whipped as their flesh peels and falls to the ground will haunt you dormant or awake. Seeing your twin hanging from a tree while their once brawn body decays to dust as the days settle will detour the most diligent deviant. "No man outrun a horse or dog for long." He tried to reason with them. "Even say you do. Where you go? Who help you? How long you survive? You swimming back to Africa?" He made valid points.

"I'z be free by morrow. I seent it. I know not where I go from here, where my next food come from, or who free with me. But I KNOW I be free." Axum, still unbothered by Jim's warnings of running and rebellion, stood firm in his belief. Several heard the sound of his voice; few dared to join his plan. Most abandoned the mere thought of it when Jim refuted with consequences. Leaving was one thing. Risking skin, limbs, and life was more than what most were willing to afford.

"You be gone morrow and back the day after at best" Jim was persistent and persuasive. "Massuh make a good example out of you. No one alive today, to see, will follow your footsteps after that happen." He said what he said and stood on it. Axum remained immovable.

"If you still have the strength to yap, I don't wanna hear no crap about you needing water or a break." The great debate was silenced as an overseer moseyed on by. He began the usual belittlement. They spoke with their eyes to one another until he left their area. Axum, full of joy and optimism, worked as if retirement was imminent and freedom in his descendant's future. If looks could kill, Jim's would have severed any and every notion of possible life outside of what he'd come to know on that peccable plantation. Wherever dreams went to die, he hoped Axum's would soon follow. They continued to toil throughout the day as time moved at a sloth's pace. Their sweat moistened the land. The salt from their perpetual perspiration could season the food of a town for months. Their labor would lay the foundation of wealth for certain whites for generations to come. They were monumental in building the essential infrastructure and economy of stolen land and made it great. The sun's blatant, constant reflection off their skin made it uncomfortable for anyone with a moral conscious to watch them for long: out of sight, out of mind. Either that or you had to convince yourself they were a different breed: their sole purpose was to serve your kind without need of their own or compassion from others.

Just before the sun began to set, and the temperature of their tegument had a chance to reset to thirty-seven degrees Celsius, Slaveholder Sam and several suited men on horseback made their way towards the enslaved. Sam was far from physically imposing, yet they feared him all the same. Whenever he was accompanied by others, and visited during "work" hours, it meant punishment, or a lesson was about to be issued. As they neared, the slaves worked like a raise was attainable. Sam called and motioned for their attention. His facial expressions squalled disturbance. He couldn't have veiled his temperament had he tried. Not that he needed to. On the land, he had the first and final say. He started to speak, "Today is a day you won't soon forget." The slaves' eyes gravitated towards Axum, but their heads never turned away from

Sam. 'Had word of Axum's plan made its way to Massuh's house?' They searched for answers within. Was he about to exercise his ultimate authority? Would an example be made that would forever stain the hearts and brains of all in attendance? "This day…this damned day in June, in the biggest, greatest state," Slavemaster Sam continued. "This nineteenth of June…"

True Story

When was God born? How did He come to be? Why'd He decide to make us in His image? Sometimes I lay in bed when the atmosphere shown on my side of the planet is mute, aside from the stars singing and the streetlights whispering, asking myself questions like these. When was His conception? Everything that has a beginning has an end date. That's how my finite brain processes reality. If He did have a start date, then how did He become who He is? Where did He get His omnipotence from? Was it Him and others of His ilk but He outlasted them and now reigns alone and supreme? Does He gain power from our worship and praise? The last one standing gets to write His narrative. Since He knows the entire story -start to finish- is this like a movie He wrote, directed, and produced? Are we merely actors of sorts, playing our part in a rerun He's binge-watching? If He isn't who the Word says He is, and atheists are correct, how were things floating around, and then BAM: all life, planets, suns, and galaxies suddenly existed? Who created the things that caused the bang!? Did they also appear and come from nothing? Why don't things still just appear from naught? We're too wonderfully complex to be a coincidence. There's too much order and alignment throughout the breathtaking cosmos for it all to be an accident. Are we the only uniquely made mortals in this immense macrocosm? Does it really matter if we aren't? We can't even get along with our neighbors or anyone different and disagreeable on Earth. Am I even alive, as we fathom, or is it all a dream? If it is my imagination, who gave me the ability to think, reckon, reason, judge, inspect, criticize, and reject? How is it possible to envision and do these things? Before all that we see came to be seen, was there a need for time? Nowadays time is all we know. It's our measurement of history. Time is "how" and what we live "by." Be on time. What time is it? What time do I need to be there? What time does it end? How much time have I wasted? How much time is left? Time how fast I can run. Time how long it takes me to get the task done. Time, time, time. It keeps going, never pauses, and is often taken for granted. Time and decay will eventually reveal our frailty. Only someone not "bound" by time can be free. Why can't we physically see God? Why can spirits see us but we lack the ability to recognize what's on the "other side"? Is there another side, or when time halts the thoughts cease to process and memories vanish? How long was God living before He created the heavenly beings? Did He get bored? Is it possible for Him to feel alone? Can He lose interest? Were the angels like us? Did they get "promoted" to paradise and replaced by us? Will we eventually be like them -the new angels- and He starts over with "new people" on a different planet? How long were Adam and Eve in Eden before the fall? Did they frequently talk with all the animals or just the shrewdest of them all? God is love. He sent His only begotten Son into a world that would hate, torture, and ridicule Him. His love is unconditional and His patience unmatched. Will He eventually rescue unbelievers from the furnace of flames? Will their wailing, gnashing of teeth, and perpetual unbearable torment eventually move Him to compassionately rescue them after they've suffered enough? After all, He's sovereign and can do as He pleases; whatever He chooses will be the correct choice, whether we concur or not. My limited mind and minimal access to knowledge, can't compute how something can subsist without a starting point, and yet here we are. No matter what others or I manifest and proclaim -happenstance or Holy design- we're here now, and one day won't be. When I toss and turn, toiling with questions throughout the night (sometimes during a flight) I seldom settle on an answer suitable for my soul. It's above my pay grade. I wasn't meant to know everything and I'm good with that. As long as I know the One who does, I can rest peacefully; He never sleeps nor slumbers. His thoughts aren't my thoughts. What does someone who knows EVERYTHING think about? Aw heck. Here I go again.

www.ingramcontent.com/pod-product-compliance
Lightning Source LLC
Chambersburg PA
CBHW031943240626
47153CB00003B/843